THE GODS OF EVERYTHING ELSE 3

REVENGE OF THE SON

T. STYLES

NATIONAL BESTSELLING AUTHOR

ARE YOU ON OUR EMAIL LIST?

SIGN UP ON OUR WEBSITE

www.thecartelpublications.com

OR TEXT THE WORD: CARTELBOOKS TO

22828

FOR PRIZES, CONTESTS, ETC.

4

PRETTY KINGS 3: DENIM'S BLUES

PRETTY KINGS 4: RACE'S RAGE

HERSBAND MATERIAL

UPSCALE KITTENS

WAKE & BAKE BOYS

YOUNG & DUMB

YOUNG & DUMB: VYCE'S GETBACK

TRANNY 911

TRANNY 911: DIXIE'S RISE

FIRST COMES LOVE, THEN COMES MURDER

LUXURY TAX

THE LYING KING

CRAZY KIND OF LOVE

SILENCE OF THE NINE

SILENCE OF THE NINE II: LET THERE BE BLOOD

SILENCE OF THE NINE III

PRISON THRONE

GOON

HOETIC JUSTICE

AND THEY CALL ME GOD

THE UNGRATEFUL BASTARDS

LIPSTICK DOM

A SCHOOL OF DOLLS

SKEEZERS

SKEEZERS 2

YOU KISSED ME NOW I OWN YOU

NEFARIOUS

REDBONE 3: THE RISE OF THE FOLD

THE FOLD

CLOWN NIGGAS

THE ONE YOU SHOULDN'T TRUST

COLD AS ICE

THE WHORE THE WIND BLEW MY WAY

SHE BRINGS THE WORST KIND

THE HOUSE THAT CRACK BUILT

THE HOUSE THAT CRACK BUILT 2: RUSSO & AMINA

THE HOUSE THAT CRACK BUILT 3: REGGIE & TAMIKA

THE HOUSE THAT CRACK BUILT 4: REGGIE & AMINA

WWW.THECARTELPUBLICATIONS.COM

THE GODS OF

EVERYTHING ELSE 3

By

T. STYLES

Library of Congress Control Number: 2022914588

ISBN 10: 1948373858

ISBN 13: 978-1948373852

Cover Design: BOOK SLUT CHICK

First Edition

Printed in the United States of America

What Up Famo,

Happy Cuffing Season! LMAO...I'm just playing, but for real, I hope you all are ready for this fall/winter season that's upon us. I hope and pray you are, and it will be a good one for you. This is my favorite time of the year!

On another note, be on the lookout for our movies, coming to a TUBI near you! We're excited about our newest movie, *"I'm Home"*, but some of our earlier projects will also be streaming on there as well. So, if you never got a chance to see them before, here's your opportunity!

Now, onto the book in hand, *THE GODS OF EVERYTHING ELSE 3*! Whenever it's been a while, I absolutely LOVE to get my Wales & Lou's fix and this installment did not disappoint! There were some cringy moments in this one, so tuck the kiddies in and dive deep! Once you get started you won't wanna stop!

With that being said, keeping in line with tradition, we want to give respect to a vet, new trailblazer paving the way or pay homage to a favorite. In this novel, we would like to recognize:

Viola Davis

Viola Davis is an AMAZING Academy, Emmy, and Tony award winning American actress who recently penned a memoir entitled, *Finding Me.* But it's her lead role in the movie, *The Woman King* for me! If you have not seen this movie, please do yourself a favor and go see it! It was outstanding and I can't wait to see it again.

Aight, my loves, catch you later!

Charisse "C. Wash" Washington
Vice President
The Cartel Publications
www.thecartelpublications.com
www.facebook.com/publishercwash
Instagram: Publishercwash
www.twitter.com/cartelbooks
www.facebook.com/cartelpublications

www.theelitewritersacademy.com
Follow us on Instagram: Cartelpublications
#CartelPublications

\#UrbanFiction

\#PrayForCece

\#ViolaDavisTheWomanKing

#THEGODSOFEVERYTHINGELSE3

PROLOGUE

The night sky was a rich purple...

Golden stars twinkled in every direction as Banks Wales stood on his beach looking at a disaster go down before his eyes. The diamond chain with a modest sized medallion sparkled against his vanilla, bronzed skin which was coated with a thin sheen of sweat due to the heat.

The sexy, salt and pepper, fully tatted up Baltimore native standing on the beach shirtless, was a beautiful contrast to the trees that outlined his property. Because as he continued to look in the distance his eyes flickered orange, due to the blaze eating up the land and brush while also threatening to destroy everything he built.

Wales Island.

His heart was breaking.

His world was shaking.

"What the fuck are you doing out here?!" Mason asked, rushing up to him. His black Versace shirt hung open, showcasing a tennis diamond necklace. "We have to get the family, get on boats and leave!" He looked at the fire which was growing quickly and back at his friend.

Although the devastation also ripped his heart he didn't care as much as Banks at the moment.

"Did you hear me? Let's go!"

Banks wanted to move.

In fact he wanted nothing more. But his feet seemed to dig deeper into the beach almost as if it were trying to swallow him whole.

This island with its glittering sand was always a dream.

The only thing he wanted more than those nearest and dearest to his heart. And now it was possible that it would be all for nothing.

"Why do things like this keep happening to me?" He turned his head in Mason's direction. "Look at my island."

Mason gazed quickly before refocusing on his friend. Almost as if the land was an afterthought. As if the island were a stranger walking by whose face he wouldn't remember the moment they bounced.

Truth be told he didn't give a fuck.

Let it all burn!

After all, although Mason enjoyed the serenity the land brought them both, nothing meant more to him than the man standing in front of him. And he wanted to ensure that he, their children, and the seeds that followed would be safe.

Banks turned his head toward him. "I can't walk away. Why can't I move?"

"Banks, I know this shit is rough! But we have to find our family and bounce! Wake the fuck up! This shit is about to be an inferno."

Banks looked down. "You know I don't complain. I try and keep my head level. But what did I do in my life not to get the dream?"

The man had selective memory, that was certain.

How quickly he'd forgotten about the bodies.

The drug lifestyle which afforded him his business.

And the way he did his son Ace by shipping him to work for the rest of his life like a slave.

"It doesn't matter!" Mason said, waving a hand dressed in a sparkling diamond watch.

"Yes it does! Once we get on those boats it will all be destroyed." He pointed at the burning land. Fire riding dry brush hopped one treetop to the next like squirrels. "Why do bad things keep happening to me? I really want to know."

It was clear that he wasn't leaving until he got his answer. So Mason did his best to give him a response.

Hunching his shoulders he said, "I don't know. But you can build all this shit back."

"That's not enough!"

"Well it's going to have to be, nigga. Because I'm not going to lose you and our family worrying about a property that you can rebuild. You've done it before, and you can do it again. Have you forgotten about Skull Island?"

He did.

Besides, in his mind it wasn't the same.

"I will never be able to rebuild this shit." Banks looked at him and Mason couldn't be sure because the heat was starting to consume him, but he swore he saw his eyes watering up. "Ever!"

Banks felt that deeply in all areas of his soul. For years he poured everything he had into the land. Making sure the blue crystal water was treasured by not allowing waste or any byproducts to be thrown in it.

By making sure the sand was cleaned and cared for four times a week by rakes.

By making sure the trees were watered and nurtured during the times the rain didn't come as planned.

And then there was his home.

He had a say so in every design element in his mansion. There wasn't a room, or a piece of furniture that didn't have his signature. Even his adult children's abodes were matters of the heart.

He adored that island and leaving it in the condition that it was now, in which fire consumed all, hurt like a mothafucka.

"Who did this shit?" Banks said through clenched teeth. "I don't get it."

"Except you do get it." Mason said, stepping a bit closer, his eyes penetrating his soul. "Don't you?"

CHAPTER ONE
TWO WEEKS EARLIER
SMUG

The moon lit up the gated property where Aliyah and Sydney were laughing inside of the kitchen of their $300,000 home in Bowie Maryland.

Aliyah was slicing fresh cheese and plating crackers while Sydney worked at popping the cork on a bottle of merlot. Both ladies looked amazing after having received spa treatments which consisted of facials, manicures, and pedicures.

Although they kept their bodies fit, their pussies clean and their clothes fashionable, they went the extra mile because it was party night. An event they did monthly to insert a little fun into their lives.

Sydney's pale skin was dusted lightly with red rouge and as she grabbed one of the crystal glasses to taste her drink, her pink lips left a print on the rim. "Wow, this is tasty."

"I told you, bitch. I know how to pick 'em."

Sydney stuffed a long strand of blonde hair behind her ear and walked closer to her friend. "I hope you don't be too bougie tonight."

Aliyah shook her head even though she was fully aware of what she meant. "You really do your best to take away the fun. Not everybody gets down like you. It doesn't mean I'm not enjoying myself."

Although Sydney didn't mind having various sexual partners to keep her heart busy, and her pussy working, Aliyah held on to the hope that Walid would return.

Shit hits differently when you realize you fucked up.

And that's exactly what she came to find when she let him go.

Originally Aliyah wanted nothing to do with him, but now she secretly wished he would fight for her love. But after breaking up with him years earlier, after discovering that he was involved in a tragic accident which resulted in her father's death, Walid decided the pain of losing her was something he wasn't willing to suffer again.

He was done.

"Are you listening?" Sydney said, nudging her out of her thoughts.

Aliyah's gold and brown faux Bohemian dreads fell to one side of her face. She stopped them from dusting the cheese and pushed the cutting board to the side. "I hear you."

"Will you have more fun tonight then? Please."

Aliyah folded her arms over her chest and leaned against the refrigerator. The tight-fitted red dress that she wore hugged her curves. The Belizean beauty said, "I'm going to tell you like I told you before. I do intend on having a good time tonight. But I'm not going to fuck a stranger just because you double dare me to."

"That is so tired!"

"What is it with you and having random sexual experiences, Sydney? I know you miss Joey but going about it this way is wrong."

Sydney placed the glass down and moved closer. Even though they were separated from their friends who laughed heavily in the living room, she could still hear their happy voices.

And she didn't want them to hear her unhappy one.

"I don't care about Joey anymore." She whispered, pointing in her face. "Nor do I want him back."

She slapped her hand away. "Except you do."

"Furthermore, I don't consider what I do to be random." She said ignoring Aliyah's statement.

"Let's put this into perspective. A few of your "friends" you met off the internet. And eventually you fucked them. Not judging but letting you know what's real."

"Aliyah, I'm very calculated with who I give my body to. You probably don't understand because you're originally from Belize."

"Please stop."

"I'm serious." She rubbed her shoulder. "We're raising two boys virtually alone. Waiting on men who want nothing to do with us to come save us again. They need to realize they had a good thing and ruined it when someone else snatches us up."

"I feel for you, I do, but Walid is a very present father and my situation ain't like yours."

"I'm not saying that he isn't."

"Then what are you saying?"

"I'm saying that we are single women who do all we can for Baltimore and Roman Wales. And it's true Walid is a good father to your boy. But the Wales family doesn't even acknowledge Roman because I made one mistake by cheating on him."

"Why won't you tell me who you cheated with?"

"It doesn't matter." Sydney paused. "Just know it was a mistake that they didn't forgive. So I don't acknowledge them either."

"I'm confused about what we're talking about now. I thought you said you didn't care about Joey."

"I don't...I mean...I don't like how they disowned him."

"I hope you didn't think having him would keep you connected to the Wales family."

"I just thought because he shares the Wales name that they would always love Roman. I guess I was wrong. And that hurts."

Aliyah felt bad for her.

Even though it was Sydney's fault that they weren't together anymore. After having sex with Joey on multiple times and not being able to have a baby, she fucked Ace and Roman was born.

As a result, the Wales family disowned her son.

But Sydney never shared this with Aliyah who remained ignorant of her secret.

"As long as we have those boys whether they acknowledge your son or not you are still connected to the Wales family. I need you to understand that because I don't think you're clear."

"I'm already over it." She waved the air.

"That's not what I'm saying. This is bigger than a relationship." She stepped closer. "They are always watching in some form. That means they own us and will disrupt our lives if they feel they can't trust us. Why else do you think they send a stipend for Roman?"

"What are you saying?"

She stepped close enough for her to smell her designer perfume. "Even if we get new niggas, they can make them disappear."

Sydney looked down.

She was getting too fucking serious.

"Can we please have fun tonight?" Sydney said firmly. "That's all I'm asking."

Aliyah nodded and picked up the cutting board.

Sydney grabbed several glasses and the bottle of wine she just popped open.

Taking a deep breath to get in the mood to play host, Sydney walked into the living room and up to the table. For a moment, her back was toward her guests. "Okay, just so we're clear we're playing truth or dare tonight!"

Everybody cheered, "Ooooooo! Can't wait!"

She turned to her right and saw Aliyah placing the cheese platter down. "See, they're excited already. So don't fuck it up."

Aliyah giggled and turned to face their guests. Suddenly her body stiffened.

"What's wrong?" Sydney muttered.

When Aliyah didn't respond, she looked closer and followed her gaze.

Sitting on the couch with the rest of her friends was Ace and his beautiful girlfriend Arbella. Her chocolate skin glittered and glowed.

If it wasn't for the dark energy he brought with him Sydney would have had him sexually all over again. He looked like he'd been through many evil situations and came out the victor.

His hair was low and the wild curls he once rocked were gone. Dark shades covered his eyes and he was wearing a pair of blue jeans and a plain white t-shirt which showed his biceps and tatts. The wardrobe was low key, but he made it look like Balenciaga.

He stroked his silky low beard and stared at them intensely.

"What's wrong?" One of their guests asked Sydney who was now trembling. Ironically enough, the guest who asked the question was sitting directly next to Ace's crazy ass and didn't know he was uninvited evil.

On the opposite side of Arbella whose long, black, luscious hair fell down the sides of her arms.

"Nothing's wrong." He said while looking directly at his baby mama, Sydney. "Right?" He said, turning his head towards Aliyah. "Now Sit."

Sydney walked over to Aliyah and softly grabbed her hand. Together they moved over to the sofa directly across from where he was propped with eight of their other friends.

"So I heard the game was truth or dare tonight?" He asked, thrusting out his chest.

"Who said that?" Sydney responded.

"You did. Just now." Aliyah whispered. "At the table."

"Oh...I...I forgot." She said with a quivering voice.

The gag was before she dealt with Walid, Ace was Aliyah's first boyfriend. It was funny how both she and Sydney had lives surrounding Ace although Aliyah didn't know about Sydney.

Arbella wrapped her arm through his and rested her head on his shoulder. Her legs crossed revealing a toned physique. She let it be known that the monster was her beautiful nightmare.

Again, Sydney and Aliyah remained silent as their bodies vibrated heavily.

"Answer the fucking question, bitches." Ace barked. "Is a game going on or not?"

"That's not nice," one of the men said.

He shot him a look that made his stomach rumble. Slowly he focused back on the ladies.

"Before I answer, I want you to know that whatever this is, will come back on you, Ace." Aliyah said softly as her body tremored.

He chuckled.

"I'm serious. If you cause drama for this family again, you'll wish you were never born."

He nodded. "You may be right." He shrugged. "But I already feel that way now."

"Wait until Banks finds out you're back."

Now their guests were aware that something deeper was going on as Aliyah and Ace continued to stare at one another from across the room.

"ARE WE PLAYING OR NOT?" He roared.

Had he not been so fine the guests would have split a long time ago. Besides, a .45 handgun rested in the back of his pants and he was fully prepared to use it.

"Um, yes, we're playing truth or dare." Sydney interrupted.

"Good. Truth or dare?" He squinted and glared.

"Tr…truth." Sydney muttered.

"Is it true that I have both of your sons tucked in the back of my trunk?"

The room screamed.

Sydney passed out.

CHAPTER TWO
CHAMELEON

The sky was clear and ice blue as Joey and Mason sat as passengers on a private jet. They would have asked Spacey, Walid or Banks to fly them but lately the three were too busy to give friends and family flights.

Which was kind of fucked up if you asked either of them.

Wearing a black linen short set with a few buttons hung loose at the top, Mason looked sturdy and like money as he thumbed through his cell phone.

Joey was across the aisle looking like a snack himself, as he readjusted the gold chain, no meddy, on his neck. "...so, like I was saying, the redhead I was telling you about busted in the room. Threw me all the way off. I don't even know how she got into the hotel."

Joey and Mason definitely had their bond intact which caused Joey to talk nonstop whenever they were alone. Plus he felt like he could tell Mason things that Banks would probably judge him on.

"Just because she wears red tracks doesn't make her a redhead but go on." He waved the air in his diamond watch cosigned.

He chuckled. "That's one man's opinion."

Mason shook his head and smiled. "Complete your story, young bull. I said I'm listening."

"Like I was saying...the redhead busted in the room. But I was with her friend in bed. And we were just getting ready to do the thing she told me she could handle on the phone."

"No kids are on this jet. Feel free to keep it a buck."

Joey chuckled. "She said she could take the dick in its entirety...no gag." He paused. "Anyway, so when she kicked the suite bedroom door down I-."

Now Mason focused on him fully. "She kicked in the door?"

"So now you're interested?"

"Any woman kicking in doors is going to be a problem for you."

"I like trouble."

"Says every dead nigga ever."

"Again, one man's opinion. Let me finish though. She kicks in the door and says, `I'm not mad that you're with my friend! I'm just mad that you cut me off. Couldn't you fuck us both?'"

"So you want me to believe she caught her friend with her slide, and she said it was cool? No way that happened."

28

"I'm telling you the truth." He raised one hand in the air.

"You been sleeping with redhead for two years." He pointed at him with a diamond studded finger. "I remember you telling me about her. I don't see a two-year extension allowing that much leeway with her friend."

"We weren't official though. I may have taken her out and showed her a good time but not on that Walid shit."

"Yeah, Walid loves wining and dining."

"She was just one of my regulars. Like you said, an extension. And since we're comparing brothers, I do pretty much what Spacey does. Keep a good beauty on speed dial and rock it until I'm done."

"So what happened after she crashed the door?"

"She had a gun. Threatened to shoot me. So I jumped up, dick still wet and calmed her down. She cried and begged me to reconsider. Next thing I know I was hitting both of 'em from the back."

Mason shook his head. "I'm not going to lie, that's about the worst story I ever heard in my life."

Joey grabbed his tequila to his right. It was actually the brand that he and Mason created. "Nah, you just don't understand a good story when you hear one." He pointed at him with a crystal glass. "Plus your mind is in the wrong place."

Mason couldn't disagree.

His mind was on other matters.

But there was a reason.

For years he had heard from Kordell, the man Banks and Mason agreed to send their adult son Ace too in Mexico for servitude. These text messages and calls put him at ease. Kordell wasn't a talkative dude. But he would at least say Ace was this...or Ace was that monthly.

But over the past few months Kordell was no longer sending updates.

And Mason was starting to wonder why.

So he had to go to Mexico to find out what the fuck was up.

"No seriously, what's on your mind?" Joey asked.

"You know what I'm thinking about."

"And we're going to check on him." He took another sip. "Why worry about it more than you need to right now?"

"I don't like to pretend to be a sorcerer. But I got a feeling that things are getting ready to turn bad for our family. Again."

"Okay. If it does, so what?"

"So what?" He frowned.

"You rich Baltimore niggas forget about your roots too easily for me." He drank what was in his glass and poured another.

"You sound crazy, youngin'."

"Think about it...there has never been a problem that we haven't gotten ourselves out of. We always come out on top, and this won't be any different if Ace is or is not in Mexico. I don't care what's going on. We invincible."

"That's where you and Banks got it fucked up. You don't understand that the boy is just like him. Able to find a way to get what he wants. And in my mind I think he wants revenge. On all of us." He took a deep breath. "I also believe Ace wants to be him."

"Be like him is not him, Uncle Mason. I don't know what we're going to find out when we land in Mexico, but I'm sure, like I said, that it's nothing we can't handle. At the end of the day what problems can he really cause for us when he's broke?"

"He could have come up on some money."

Joey chuckled. "But not Wales money."

Mason thought about that sentence.

To be fair, there was a difference.

Banks had billions at this point. And although Mason's money was a little right it was nothing compared to his dear friend. And he knew Ace's funds wouldn't be either.

But history had shown that more trouble had been caused by broke niggas than those with big money ever could. So he felt no one should underestimate Ace.

After all he was still a Wales.

"We're landing, sirs." The pilot said from the cockpit.

Mason saluted him.

"We good," Joey told Mason with a smile. "Trust me, Unc."

Mason nodded.

When the plane landed the first thing they did was get into their chauffeured Maybach for a ride to Kordell's house. Kordell lived in one of the most lavish estates in the country. Only millionaires could afford to reside with such prestige. Sadly enough not many of them were native men.

For instance, Kordell was from the hood in America.

But, when the driver pulled up to the property, what they saw caused Mason and Joey to cover their waists where their guns rested.

Because there was nothing luxurious about this compound.

The property was unkempt.

The grass was as high as kneecaps.

Wild animals seemed to hop about as if they owned the spot. And trash piled up along the driveway.

It was so bad they couldn't go any further by car.

They had to explore on foot if they wanted to get answers.

Hyper curious, Joey and Mason eased out of the car and closed the doors. Standing next to the vehicle they looked at the doorway in the horizon.

"What you think this is about?" Joey questioned looking at rodents peering at them from the high grass.

"I don't know. But let's go find out."

Walking further away from their driver, who stood by their vehicle ready to blast anything that meant them harm, they made it to the front door of Kordell's trash ass estate.

Knocking once they waited for someone to open the residence and explain why a millionaire lived in a garbage dump all of a sudden.

Slowly the large double black doors opened and an elderly woman greeted them. "Who are you?" Her accent was Mexican which was on brand for the beautiful country. "What do you want?"

"Is Kordell here?" Mason said.

She looked down and back at Mason and Joey who immediately knew something was going on.

"Are you Mr. Wales?"

They remained cool and composed although they were uncomfortable that it appeared as if they were expected.

"Where is Kordell?" Mason repeated.

"Please wait here. Let me get his wife."

She walked away looking back once.

With the door open, they inhaled the grossest odors stemming from the property and it made them cover their noses.

It smelled of spoiled food, stacked trash and rotten flesh.

Did she kill Kordell?

Before long a woman who was on the last legs of her beauty presented herself. Her scraggly black hair was scraped up into a bun and her eyes were sunk within her skull. It looked like she hadn't eaten in months.

At first, despite gazing at Mason, she appeared to look through him in a glazed over fashion. Suddenly she recognized who he was.

34

"How did you know where I lived?" She closed her robe tighter. "Why did you come to my home?"

"Where is my son?" He rocked on his feet.

"It wasn't a son that you left with us." She glared, guilt covering her words. "Remember? We paid for him. That made him a slave."

Joey stepped forward to get physical, but Mason pushed him back slightly with a flat palm. "Where is my son? I won't ask you politely again."

She took a deep breath. "I don't know. Truly I don't."

Mason looked at Joey and suddenly Joey grew uneasy.

Maybe Mason was right after all.

The bitch called Trouble wanted the Wales' again.

The family was clearly cursed.

"When was the last time you saw him?"

She cleared her throat. "Two years ago."

Mason was furious. "But Kordell had been texting me, telling me he was in Mexico!" He pointed at the ground. "It's only been a month since his messages stopped coming."

"I found out later he left. And I'm sorry."

Mason was growing angrier. "Tell me more."

"At first no one knew where Ace was. He seemed to just vanish." She crossed her arms over her chest. "And then word got back to me and Kordell that Nicolas Rivera had taken him."

Mason's heart thumped. "Nicolas Rivera?"

"I thought he was dead, Unc!" Joey asked Mason.

"Exactly!" Mason said, looking at her harder. He felt like he and Banks had been taken for their paper. Speaking mostly to Joey he said, "As a matter of fact, murdering Nicolas was why Banks set up Kordell's business, making him a legal millionaire. He felt he owed him a debt based on taking Nicolas' life. Now we finding out it was all a lie."

"He thought he was dead too." She whispered. "Truly. But evil don't die. We all know that."

Mason was so angry he was trembling. Had he known the man was alive he would have never sanctioned Ace living in Mexico. He knew Nicolas' rage for the Wales and Louisville families ran deep.

"Don't worry, Nicolas is dead now though." She continued.

"How?"

"He died of natural causes."

Mason was pissed.

Why should he get a knight's death after all the havoc he wreaked in the world?

She had been better off not even telling him that shit.

"Once word got back where he was buried, his enemies dug him up even though Ace did a good job trying to hide his body," she continued to rattle as if she couldn't wait for this moment.

"Wait...Ace buried him? Why would he care what happened with Nicolas?" Joey responded.

"Because he became a good friend to him. Some say he came to love Nicolas like a father. I don't know if it was true but if it is, you and your family are in danger. Nicolas was grimey but he was very smart."

Joey took a deep breath and shook his head. "Here we go again." He looked at Mason. "You were right after all, Unc. Bet the shit feels good huh?"

Nah.

It didn't feel good.

"Where is Kordell?" Mason responded.

Suddenly she began to sob. "A month back, I came home to find his throat sliced and his body covered with dimes."

Mason's blood felt as if it ran cold.

When Banks gave Ace to Kordell, he sold him for a dime. The money wasn't necessary but when Ace once told Banks he would give up his luxurious lifestyle for a dime, Banks thought it would be fitting to sell him into servitude to Kordell for the same price.

Now it would come back to bite them all.

"Who killed your husband Kordell?" Joey asked.

"I don't know...but we have our ideas." She looked harder. "Don't we?"

The next question Mason wanted to know had him struggling to release the words. "Do you know where Ace is now?"

"No. But if I were you I would start preparing for the worst. He's coming. Trust me, he's coming!"

CHAPTER THREE
FLEWED OUT

Walid was flying a helicopter with his girl of the moment. They were going to a destination only he knew.

He looked slick with the diamond in his ear that sparkled due to the glowing control panel bouncing from below. The silk short sleeve black shirt with black printed roses was opened at the top.

As she watched him handle the skies, his gray slacks which low-key showed his dick print had her horny when she gazed downward.

As he busied himself with the control system, he could feel her eyes on him, watching his every move. Light Brown was the type of girl who didn't get a man like this, so she was in awe.

Wondering why he chose her.

Wondering how she could be so lucky.

Spending most of her life on the pole, she resigned herself to having to accept what came her way. Most were drug dealers. Overworked nine to-fivers who felt she owed them something after coming home exhausted.

She never knew "something better" existed. And now that she found a real-life prince, she didn't want the moment to end.

"Why you keep looking at me like that, girl?" He said as he continued to pilot the helicopter. "Don't make me slide over there."

Light Brown readjusted the tight-fitting red dress she wore and brushed her brown hair over her shoulder. Real money made her nervous. "If you slide over here, who gonna fly?" She giggled.

"I can handle both of you with one hand." He looked at her and she immediately felt less than. "Trust me."

He scratched the part in between his long French braids.

Why did he have to be so fine? So sexy. She thought.

Looking down, she said, "I can't believe you chose me."

He glared. "I need you to stop doing that shit. You have to recognize who you are. Don't wait on a nigga like me to tell you. You may not always get that opportunity."

"I know what you're saying is true. But when you're told so long you only deserve one thing, getting something this good doesn't add up. It's going to take a little time. But if you stay around maybe I'll begin to understand. Maybe I'll start believing you."

He winked.

Walid was a good dude, but he definitely had a kink.

Part of the thing that got him going was choosing women in environments that weren't accustomed to the type of money he had in his possession. Only to douse them with thousands.

Walid was not his father.

But he had access to the millions given to him in a trust and in his bank account. He didn't have to work a day in his life if he didn't desire. So the type of work that brought him joy was picking a girl from the hood, flying her around and sliding money on her to make her shine in his light.

Whenever he did this it was like he was experiencing his wealth all over again.

Half million-dollar car rides.

Helicopter flights.

Hermes. Fendi. Louis Vuitton shopping sprees.

He liked to splurge on a rough from the streets.

Unconsciously, when he did this, he was saving Aliyah all over again whenever he picked a female from the hood.

He was done with his son's mother.

That much was true. But his thoughts went on her daily.

Although she would never be able to tell.

"Where we going?" She whispered. "I'm getting so excited I can't contain myself."

"I said I got you for your birthday. That means I got you for your birthday. So you're gonna have to trust me."

Suddenly they begin to lower.

The skyline appeared to light up as if it were waiting on their arrival.

When he landed the helicopter on top of a luxury apartment building he owned in Washington DC, he opened the door and immediately four armed men rushed to help them out.

Neither the royal family on the first family could fuck with his level of protection.

He loved his security.

Just like Banks.

It made him safe.

In fact, he spent more on security than his brothers.

He learned from the best.

Earlier that day he had taken Light Brown to get her hair done and he also spent $7,000 on the red dress that sparkled lightly while hugging her curves that she was wearing tonight. Before that moment he presented it to her in a large black box with a ribbon that matched the shirt he was wearing.

She almost fainted at the designer threads.

Several times he caught her pinching herself, but he didn't let on. She was trying to see if what was happening was real.

It was.

While spinning on that pole, she had successfully gained a billionaire's attention.

"Ms. Brown..." Holding out his arm she threaded hers through his as they walked on the roof and threw a door which was held by another one of his employees.

Walid had an apartment in the penthouse of his building, and he stayed there whenever he was in town to see his son Baltimore. Within the luxurious property, there was a banquet room which was totally surrounded by floor to ceiling windows overlooking the city.

It was there that he was about to blow her mind.

As they made their way through the lobby padded with gold and red carpeting, they seemed to glide up to a large elevator door which opened smoothly. Once inside, Walid touched the panel and the door closed.

Had anybody else tried to use the elevator it wouldn't work because it was sensitive to his fingerprint only.

Hitting the button to go down after a few seconds, the doors opened again. The moment they were ajar, familiar faces screamed happy birthday in Light Brown's direction.

Tears formed in the wells of her eyes.

Walid, with the help of her friends, had taken the time to make sure everyone she cared about was in that room. He even invited a few women who were on the fringes of their friendship because he wanted to do her the honor of rubbing it in their faces.

She landed a billionaire.

Let the world see that shit!

Based on the treatment she was given; you would think this was his main girl. But it was far from that fact. He had only known her for six months.

And considering his track record, it didn't mean he would know her for much more. He was known for splurging and then dropping a stipend in his absence enough to pay for one year of college or fund a business if he so chose.

But they could never have his heart.

"Walid, this is beautiful!"

He walked her over to a table that was filled with boxes from Hermes, Chanel, and Louis Vuitton. There was food on the other side of the banquet and music consisting of her favorite songs blasted from the ceiling speakers. He got these hits from the playlist on her iPhone which meant everything that boomed would be her favorite.

For now, the anthem, *Whole Lotta Money* by *Bia* rocked the room.

She was shaking, she was on cloud ten.

Standing over top of her he whispered in her ear, "Happy birthday, Light."

He gripped her with one arm, and she melted into his body. "I can't believe you did this for me."

"I did."

"I love you."

Damn...

Wrong words.

Walid was a good man, but love was not something he would participate in anymore. Just hearing the statement put him on edge and softened his dick.

It made him uncomfortable.

Separating from him she said, "Did you hear what I said? I love you."

"I heard you." He managed to hold a smile but didn't tell her what she wanted to hear.

After all, it would be a lie.

"Go hang out with your friends, shawty. We will do us later."

"Are you sure?"

"Get your fine ass over there." He slapped her ass with a hand wearing a wrist full of ice.

A smile stayed on his face until she didn't look back anymore.

As she walked away, he allowed her friends and family to close in on her with congratulations and well wishes.

When he could no longer see her in the crowd, he strolled back to the elevator, his security guards right behind him.

Within fifteen minutes he was back on the roof leaving Light Brown alone.

Some people may think it was cold leaving her on her birthday.

But he didn't care.

They could suck his big dick.

He would never allow love to enter his heart again.

Just as the helicopter lifted off the pad, he received a text from Mason.

DROP WHATEVER BITCH YOU GOT AND
COME HOME NOW!

CHAPTER FOUR
BILLIONS

B anks and Faye Wales sat across from the owners of Foriding Energy Services.

This was billion-dollar shit and wasn't reserved for those who couldn't understand losing or gaining hundreds of millions of dollars at a time.

But the Wales family definitely knew this lifestyle.

And they fuckin' loved it.

After creating an app that would provide customers big and small with the places to purchase affordable oil or access to charging stations for electric vehicles, they had easily slid into the heavyweight game.

This one deal alone would make Banks Wales as wealthy as Elon Musk.

With a document in front of him that would push him into another tax bracket, he looked over at his beautiful wife. "This all you."

"*We* did it," she said, her hair in luscious black locks that dripped down the sides of her face.

"Nah, you did that."

She was so happy she couldn't be still.

She always dreamed of having a plush ass lifestyle. And her youth made her feel it would take forever. But when Banks hit her up when he needed to make Kordell a legal millionaire, he remembered meeting her at one point.

She created the app.

He helped Kordell.

And the rest was her fairytale.

After signing first, he slid the paperwork to his young wife. She had become instrumental to Banks' money game and for foreplay they did things like provide up-and-coming entrepreneurs in Baltimore with the bankroll necessary to spearhead their businesses and create new lives for themselves.

It was about spreading the wealth.

They definitely gave back.

When the ink was dry the COO of FES extended his hand and shook them both. "Welp, this is a game changer, Mr. and Mrs. Wales."

"We know," Banks bragged.

He hugged his wife and kissed her lips.

She shivered because he was so fucking fine.

Daddy Warbucks type shit but richer, browner, and finer.

"We have one more document we need you to sign and then we're done for the day."

"Okay. But me and my wife have to do something right quick. Keep the ink wet. I'm gonna get into something else."

He pulled out her chair, grabbed her hand and they exited the boardroom. Conversations about how they liked to fuck after inking deals ran rampant in the business world. And so the executives of FES knew they had to wait for them to finish doing their thing to get the deal finalized.

Walking to his office, they entered and closed the door.

"I love you." She spoke. "I can't believe we did this. I can't believe you found me again and changed my life."

He picked her up and placed her on his desk. Pulling her panties down, he raised her skirt. Since nothing got him off more than making millions it was time to show his gratitude.

Getting on his knees, he pushed her legs apart. The smell of her sweet pussy greeted him and he parted her soft hair free lips. Running his tongue over her clit and deep into her canal it didn't take long for her to get oily.

After all she got off on making money too.

Grabbing the back of his head she pushed deeper and harder on his tongue. Her entire body trembled as she felt herself about to explode. Whether he was going down or fucking her from behind, Banks was a generous lover.

And she felt happy to have him as her husband.

They were just ready to go all in when he received an urgent text message from Mason.

CRAWL THE FUCK OUT THE PUSSY AND COME HOME NOW!

The night sky entered the living room where the magnificent beach was in view. Rain hadn't fallen in weeks and so things were already tense for many people living on the surrounding islands.

But this wasn't about the visuals.

This meeting was about betrayal.

Kordell's wife stood in the middle of the floor in the living room in the mansion on Wales Island and she felt her life was on the line. She didn't want to be there. But Mason and Joey made her come back to explain what was going down with Ace.

To forewarn them about the danger slithering their way.

On the sofa sat Minnesota Wales who was holding her two-year-old niece, Sugar Wales whom Blakeslee, her sister, gave birth to without knowing the father due to her whorish ways. Her miniature, English bulldog Pit-Pat sat in her other arm.

Blakeslee was also in the building.

Sitting on the floor with her legs gacked open, she was wearing a white bikini top and black shorts so skimpy they showed her pussy and butt print. Then there was the makeup. Her lips were covered with so much red lipstick she could kiss a hundred niggas and not need a retouch.

Actually she'd done that before.

Every now and again Mason's eyes would fall on her, but she never seemed to notice. Her mind was too busy with how whatever the meeting was about, may fuck up her lifestyle.

Spacey, Joey, and Walid sat closely to one another, as if needing each other for physical support.

On floors scattered throughout, sat 17-year-old Patrick Louisville who was Mason's grandson and 16-year-old Bolt Louisville who was Mason's son.

Eighteen-year-old Riot Wales, who was Spacey's only son, was also present. Ordinarily they wouldn't allow the younger ones to attend such a serious meeting. But it was important that they understood the family they were born into.

It was giving billionaires with criminal tendency vibes.

Banks and Mason sat in their own plush recliners as everyone in the room looked upon Kordell's widow for answers.

"So you're telling me that Kordell lied and took my money." Banks said plainly, while pulling on a cigar.

"I don't know the arrangement you had with him. I'm just giving you the info I have today. And I'm sorry for all this confusion."

"You did know." Banks corrected her, pointing her way with the cigar. His shirt hung open revealing his diamond necklace and winged tattoo. "Because it was important for me to make sure that you were with this situation before I sent Ace. Because I didn't want to take the risk of Ace popping up somewhere else."

"I swear to you I knew nothing. Kordell did his best not to involve me. I didn't find out he was your son until after Ace had gone missing."

"So what made him tell you?" Spacey glared. "Since you were so fucking innocent."

"Because he needed me to know in case you showed up. And to be honest I wanted it that way. I mean look at this? Now having all this information, I feel like I'm responsible for Ace not being around."

Banks stood up, pressed the fire out of his cigar and paced rapidly. Every time he moved past the moonlight from the open window his diamond necklace would glow.

"When was the last time you saw him?" Mason questioned.

"To be honest when I saw him originally, had someone told me he was your son I would not have believed them. He was soiled." She shook her head. "Dirty. He looked nothing like the son of a billionaire."

"Because he's not the son of a billionaire." Banks said, pointing at the floor.

"Facts." Spacey responded.

"Not facts." Minnesota interjected. "Just because you're beefing with him, father doesn't mean he is not a Wales. I thought you understood this."

"I don't have to understand shit! He decided to be outside of this family the moment he betrayed us. So I gave him his wishes and his wings. Besides, before I sent

54

him to Mexico, we all agreed." He was speaking to Mason, Minnesota, Spacey, Walid and Joey, less they develop a conscience. "The alternative was death. So don't backpedal now."

"I would never backpedal." Minnesota spoke up.

"Good! He was dangerous!"

"Facts," Spacey said.

"Like I said he is no longer a part of this family!" Banks continued. "And everybody in this room had better remember that shit if you wanna keep your lifestyle."

"He is still our son!" Mason said loudly. "And the way you handled this was sickening. I told you we should have known more about him and his whereabouts in Mexico, but you were satisfied with the few phone calls and texts that Kordell sent."

He frowned. "You didn't seem to have a problem with it when he tried to kill Walid."

Riot, Bolt and Patrick all looked at one another.

It was the first they heard of such things.

"That's not true! How many times have I come to you and begged you to verify that he still had eyes on Ace?"

"So, this my fault now?" He pointed to himself.

"Yes. Because you've been so focused on building businesses with your *pretty young wife* that you didn't understand that a threat was looming."

"Keep my wife's name out your mouth."

"Nah, nigga, we need to talk about this shit," Mason continued pointing at the floor. "Because if you love and trust her so much, why isn't she in this meeting?"

Silence.

"Like I said, we could never have the peace we desire behind what we all did to Ace. Revenge has a lot of passion. Ace has a lot of passion. Do you believe me now?"

"What did the nigga do besides possibly leave Mexico?"

"We'll see," Mason said. "Won't we?"

Banks went to make himself a drink.

Everybody in the room said, "I want one too."

Not feeling like being a maid, he hit the button on the wall and his butler came quickly. By the time he left everyone had glasses of whiskey on the rocks.

He even allowed the boys to have a little wine in their sippy cups.

Banks breathed deeply. "Somebody's going to take you home. I appreciate the information you've given me tonight."

"No problem. I really hope I was helpful, but I fear I didn't know enough." She looked down. "I hate to ask this question. But is it possible that you could give me some money? When Kordell died, they took everything. And those who owe won't give me the funds. So me and my children have nothing."

"Fuck you talking about? Are you really pushing me for cash?"

"It's just that-."

"I don't have anything for you." Banks said. "Your husband dropped the ball and that put me in a bind. I won't be put in another one again. Not for his bitch or his kids."

Everybody in the room felt that it was cold, but no one expected anything different from Banks either.

He was starting to embody what it meant to be a shrewd businessman.

And a shrewd human being.

She shook her head and walked toward the door slowly, and Pit-Pat chased her down the hall.

"Minnie, get that fucking dog!" Banks yelled, embarrassed upon hearing the woman screaming down the corridors.

She handed Spacey the baby and ran after her dog. A few minutes later she returned to reclaim her seat and Sugar.

When everyone was together again, Banks looked at his family.

"I know everyone is scared." He walked around the room, sure to lay eyes on every single family member. "But there is no reason to be. It would be impossible for Ace to come to this island. Remember? You can only get on our land by boat or plane. And Nicolas didn't leave him any money."

"But what if he did?" Mason said.

"Then he would be shot in the sea or blown out of the air. His choice."

Mason was heated. "I think you're making a mistake by not taking this situation seriously. Yet again." Mason pointed his way. "We need to find out where he's resting his head."

"Mason, I'm done giving this shit energy. I just made enough money to make my eighth generation independently wealthy. So, you can do what you wanna. But leave me out the broke nigga shit." He winked. "Excuse me, but I'm going to see about my *pretty young wife*."

Banks grabbed his glass and bopped out of the lounge in that rich nigga stroll, leaving them alone.

CHAPTER FIVE
THE VIG

fonts in that room.

Ace sat in the living room of a brothel house that Aliyah used to prostitute herself inside of before he returned from Mexico.

Now it was taken over by him.

No doubt the ladies were still allowed to work. Besides, he admired them for getting their paper.

It was the hustle for him.

Pretty bitches.

Some knotted with cellulite.

Others, as tight as porcelain dolls.

He loved it all.

As long as he was getting his cut.

Propped in a single large brown recliner that had seen better days, the way his body melted into the tattered material, it looked like he was seated on a throne.

His lightly tinted shades covered his eyes. And the black button-down shirt exposed his chiseled chest and his tats.

When Ocean, the brothel's owner, tried to reject his offer for 10% of the profit the brothel gained, he readjusted his tinted shades and said, "Cool. Sorry to bother you."

Later that night, strange men ended up in her home after having broken windows and doors to make themselves comfortable in their beds.

On her living room floor.

Just everywhere.

She was stressed the fuck out.

And what was she going to do? Call the police.

Ace, or Cabello as he preferred to be called by strangers, definitely hung out with the darker element and it was only on his word that they dispersed and left her home.

Later that night, she said, "Okay...ten percent."

"Nah...now it's twenty. You fucked the other price up."

She reluctantly agreed believing shit would get worse.

This night, Aliyah and Sydney sat in front of Ace while prostitutes walked around them scantily dressed, with various strangers in tow. A few of the Johns wanted to drop the whores for Aliyah and Sydney until Ace shot them looks to kill.

These women weren't for sale.

Not now anyway.

"What is this place?" Sydney questioned. "Why would you bring my boy here?"

He leaned forward. "It doesn't matter. The only thing that matters is what will happen next."

"Why did you have to take our sons?" She trembled. "They don't have anything to do with any of this!"

"First off, one of those sons is mine." He spoke, nodding with assurance.

Aliyah laughed. "What you talking about?"

He frowned. "So you disrespecting now?"

"How is Roman or Baltimore your son?"

"Wait, you mean to tell me you were living with her all this time and you didn't know that Roman is my seed?" He gripped his dick.

Aliyah glared at Sydney who looked away.

"Is this true?"

Silence.

"Answer me, Sydney!"

"Yes." Her chest deflated as if she were a hot air balloon and someone poked her with a pin.

"Is this the reason they cut you off?"

"Y…Yes."

"Why wouldn't you tell me this?"

"Because I'm ashamed. Of how everything went down. Would you even have been my friend had you known the truth? I mean look at how you're looking at me right now. Like you're disgusted."

She was disgusted.

"You would not have remained my friend. I know it. Be honest." She cried, wiping her eyes with tight fists.

Aliyah couldn't say with certainty. But it definitely explained why the family wanted nothing to do with her.

Or Roman.

But later for her white ass.

Focusing back on Ace she said, "How long are you going to keep my son here? Because you and I both know if you keep him this will start a war."

"It will start a war, but not for the reasons you think."

"What you want from me?" She said, throwing her hands up in the air. "I have been written off!"

"I want you to get back with Walid."

She leaned backward slowly. "Get back with Walid?" She frowned. "What sense does that make?"

"So now you going to play dumb?"

"Ace, I'm being sincere. Walid wants nothing to do with me. He said that several times to my face."

He laughed just as another woman took two men upstairs to pleasure. She was built like a statue.

When she was gone he said, "You want me to believe that the same nigga who took you from me doesn't want you anymore?"

Arbella got up and left.

Although he knew she felt a way about how they were once childhood sweethearts, he hated that she could not control her emotions.

"I don't care what my brother told you. I would bet money on the fact that he still wants you. You just have to give him a reason to take you back."

"It won't work, I swear to God."

"I'm not going to sit here and try and convince you of what I know to be true. But I will say this. That nigga's heart still beats for you. I feel it as if he were me. That's the way it is with twins."

"Even if I did convince him, what happens next?"

He glared. "I don't have to tell you what happens next, bitch. But I do say you have to do what I tell you." He pointed at the scratched wooden floor.

"What about my son?" Sydney interjected; wild blonde hair scattered everywhere. "I see why you want her involved. But none of this makes sense to me."

"So you're trying to get my son hemmed up?" Aliyah asked her. "Because the other day we were all best friends and now you don't care about what happens to my child?"

"You know I care about that boy as much as you do. At the same time this is the truth. Roman doesn't have anything to do with this."

"First let me say this," Ace said to Sydney. "When it comes to your son I have just as much say as you. And whether or not I allow him to live with you will be based on what's done over the next couple of days."

"What does that mean?"

He ignored Sydney and looked straight at Aliyah. "You will make him fall in love with you again."

"And what if it doesn't work?"

"Then I'll make my nephew my son. And you will never see him again."

Arbella was crying and sniffling on the bed when Ace walked into the room. It was the same room she used to sell her body before he returned to her. But for now it would be their home until his final destination.

He looked down at her with disdain. "What the fuck you doing out there?"

She sat up and looked at him. "Why you been walking funny lately?"

"I asked what the fuck you doing?" He said ignoring her.

"What you talking about, Cabello?"

"You're playing yourself weak."

"You know what, can you please stop talking to me right now."

He moved closer.

Almost as if he glided.

In fact, he was so close he could feel her body heat as she sat on the edge of the bed. Not to be moved, he stood firmly like a tree. "Never talk to me like that again. I haven't laid hands on you since I been back. Don't make me forget the reason why."

"How am I supposed to take any of this?"

"You said you would ride for me. This is riding."

"Why do you take my discomfort as me not riding? I'm a woman. And I have a right to how I feel. Whether you like it or not. I don't understand what the problem is with me being hurt about you talking to a woman you once wanted."

"We spoke in detail about what needed to happen in order for us to get on with our lives. I told you my plan to get my son and then some."

66

"You mean in order for *you* to get on with your life. All I ever wanted was *you*. I have you. I will be good with just that."

"Stop lying!" He said, slamming his fist into his hand. "You came from money before you started selling your body. Which means you want money now. You don't want this broke shit for yourself, and I won't have it for a woman on my arm."

He was right.

"I forgave the past. With you giving another nigga your body to make ends meet as a whore. But I won't settle into it for the future. We need that money. And I need a woman who understands that."

"It's about so much more than the money isn't it? With the Wales'."

He was done suffering having to give explanations. "Never react like that again, Arbella. I'm warning you."

CHAPTER SIX
ATTRACTION

Blakeslee was in her bedroom with her friend Sharon.

Sharon was holding Minnesota's puppy as he yipped, yapped, and pissed in her arms. Despite it being very gross, she acted as if she didn't care.

They were rehashing what Ace's return meant for Blakeslee and as they sat on the floor in her bedroom, each grew giddy with excitement.

Sharon, who was a dark Belizean girl, 24, with large eyes, looked at her friend with curiosity. She had long dirty dreads that rolled down her back which she refused to clean on a regular basis believing it would take away her power.

And so they stank whenever she moved around too much like now.

Sharon was mysterious for two reasons.

First she considered herself to be a Shaman. Someone with powers to do anything they wanted to anybody with a spell. Although her process didn't always seem on record with what was known of shamans in the past, she had a lot of confidence in her acts.

And Blakeslee had confidence in her which made them a match.

The next thing that made Sharon weird was her obsession with Minnesota's puppy, Pit-Pat. And whenever she came over the house she would find a way to get the dog in her hands.

A few times Minnesota had to catch her from walking out the mansion with the animal and Sharon claimed she always forgot.

She didn't forget.

She was trying to steal the bitch.

"Tell me again about your brother Ace." Sharon said. "Because he sounds like he has a big dick!"

"He is so fine! Like you heard, he's also dangerous. But he would never hurt me."

"How do you know? Everyone else seems so scared."

She thought about how close they were when they were younger. And she also thought about how she ruined his trust by bringing men into his penthouse when she lived with him before he was sent to Mexico.

Despite it all she was certain that he still loved her.

And he would never harm her.

"He won't put me in danger! Trust me!"

"Well what's up with Mason?" Sharon asked.

"What are you talking about?"

"I think he really likes you. I saw how he looked at you across the room when I was peeping in from the hallway. Is there more between you two then you told me about?"

"If my father would've caught you staring in the meeting you would be dead."

"Well it's a good thing he didn't. Now answer the question."

"At one point I thought Mason was feeling me. But whenever I come around he leaves quickly so I was wrong. Plus he's my father's best friend so–."

"You blind, Blakeslee." She paused. "And if I were you, I would pay attention to that man. I know your father doesn't really like you so–"

"Who said that?"

"Look, I told you I had powers. And I see the energy around him. He doesn't feel you."

Blakeslee believed her but it was still hard to hear. Because she didn't know why Banks didn't care for her.

Sharon moved closer, her warm breath fluttering her eyelids. "Link yourself to Mason. If you do, I believe you'll be as powerful as your father if not more. Because even though Banks doesn't want to listen to anyone, I can tell he respects Mason."

"How can I link myself to him?"

"First...start some shit around here. Play the victim. If I'm right Mason will come to the rescue."

The Triad, consisting of Patrick, Riot and Bolt sat in Riot's room after having just heard that Ace was not where everyone thought he should be.

In Mexico.

Away from family.

"I don't know where I thought he went but I definitely didn't think he was in Mexico." Bolt said. "I'm not worried. Ace is mean. But Uncle Banks will make sure he can't hurt us."

"You don't know that for sure." Riot responded.

"I don't have facts, but it seems like every time somebody tries to take us out, it's a problem. For them not us. Uncle Banks has enough money to make everything go away."

"That's true but he did seem worried tonight." Riot responded. "That's because he knows how dangerous

Uncle Ace can be. You heard Mason. This is very serious."

"You a hater." Patrick laughed. "Against your own grandfather at that."

"What are you talking about?" Riot said.

"Every time we talk about how powerful this family is, you start talking scared."

Bolt laughed.

"My mother says they aren't moving smart," Riot said. "So I'm just–."

"Scared!" Patrick continued cutting him off.

"You letting your American mother get in your head." Bolt giggled.

"I don't care where Ace is at this point." Patrick continued. "He turned his back on his family and anybody who turns their back on this family is dead to us. I'm riding with Uncle Banks."

"I think you're the one that's confused."

"How? I once heard Uncle Banks got rid of a whole town that tried to hurt us." Bolt continued. "And he would do the same thing."

"Against his own son though?" Riot responded.

"All of y'all sound dumb." Blakeslee said entering the room with Sharon.

Blakeslee and Sharon hung in the doorway before walking further into Riot's room.

"Ace is very smart and he is dangerous." She continued. "And because father cut him off financially and didn't allow his twin brother to talk to him, he's probably looking to get back any way he can."

"So? What part of that means that Uncle Banks can't handle him?" Patrick questioned.

"To be honest I don't know who would win. When Ace lived with us some people said he reminded them of father. But what y'all should be remembering or thinking about is the fact that if something were to happen to father or Mason only his blood relatives would be financially set. The rest of y'all would have to go back to the States and get it from the mud."

The Triad looked at one another.

"What are you talking about?" Patrick said.

"Yeah, what are you talking about?" Mason asked upon hearing her words to the group of young boys.

Blakeslee was scared.

Didn't see him in the room.

"I'm just saying with Ace showing back up there isn't a lot of security financially if something were to happen to either of you. So that means the Louisville's would have to go back to the States. Right?"

73

"Banks would never allow something to happen to me and not have shit set." Mason said confidently.

"But what about us?" Patrick said. "Me and Bolt. Would we be good too? Or is what she saying right?"

Suddenly they all begin to speak loudly, mostly out of fear.

"Lower your voices!"

Mason did his best to try and calm them down, but no one was listening. They spoke louder and louder until Banks, who was on his way to find Riot, entered and saw the commotion.

"I said shut the fuck up little niggas!" Mason said.

The room silenced.

"What's going on?" Banks asked.

Everyone remained mute.

"I asked a question."

Blakeslee took a deep breath. "I was just telling them that if something were to happen to you and Mason, only your bloodline is protected. Not the Louisville's."

"So what? Doesn't mean that my bloodline won't look out for the Louisville's."

Upon getting confirmation Mason's brow furrowed.

"But we ain't dead yet." Banks said, trying to make light. "So stop all that worrying. We gonna be fine." He looked at Riot. "Come with me. I want you to look at the website we're creating for sneakerheads."

Mason looked at Patrick, Bolt, Blakeslee, and Sharon. He wasn't feeling the response one bit.

"Everything will be okay," he said to Patrick and Bolt even though he wasn't sure. "I would never let anything happen to myself without setting you up first." He walked out.

"Now do y'all believe me?" Blakeslee giggled before leaving out with Sharon following.

CHAPTER SEVEN
DAYS LATER
BIRTHDAY BITCH

Blakeslee switched into Banks' office with a smile on her face. Her birthday was coming in a few months and she had some ideas for things she wanted. But first it was time to ask for an increase of her stipend.

"Father, I was wondering if–."

The moment he heard her voice, he glared up at her from his paperwork. She was an awful mother, and a troublemaker so he wondered why she had the nerve to ask him anything. "What's up with you not feeding Sugar when you keep her with you overnight?"

She was confused. "Wait, what you talking about?"

"You know exactly what I'm talking about. Whenever Minnesota gets her, she hasn't eaten, been cleaned or anything."

She stood before him, her chin trembling. "I don't understand why you coming at me this way. Sugar loves me."

"You aren't a good mother, Blakeslee. And people are noticing."

"What about you and what you did to Ace? You not a good mother either."

He rose from his desk, knocking things over. "Fuck you just say?"

"I'm...I didn't mean it." She looked down.

"Since you care about Ace so much, think about what happened to him."

"You would do that to me?" She started blinking rapidly.

"I have no problem getting rid of a family member. I'm starting to think that if I do decide to clean house, the next person to go will be you."

Thinking about Ace had her stomach churning.

Although she knew she was trouble as far as Banks was concerned, she held onto the hope that because she was a Wales that he would never cut her off.

But it was becoming clearer that Banks did not care for her. And that hurt her greatly.

She stepped a little deeper inside. Her shoulders dropped. "Why do you hate me so much? What is it about me that makes you never say anything good?" She began to cry.

"You can stop your fucking tears. They don't work in this office. They don't work on me. I'm not for your games. You can try it on the niggas you fuck instead!"

"Father, I love you. I-."

"Get out! Now!"

Blakeslee took off running and crying on her way down the hall. She was so upset that she ran into Sharon who was holding Minnesota's dog again. She was looking out of the window, in the distance.

When she heard her pleas, she said, "What's wrong? What happened?"

"He hates me! And I don't understand why!"

"Do you think it was because of what you said to the boys? About them having to sell dick to make a living back in the States if Mason or Banks dies."

"I never said that! Anyway, you told me to start trouble."

"And I want you to. Just didn't seem like Mason was gonna rescue you, that's all."

"He probably doesn't like me either. And can you please put that dog down. It's staring at me."

It was true.

She put the dog down and said, "Stay."

The dog shit, pissed and ran off.

She was about to take off after it until Blakeslee grabbed her hand.

"He's getting away!"

"It's not your dog."

78

Sharon glared. "I need to protect him."

"Sharon, what are you talking about! Leave his ass alone! You my friend!"

Sharon rolled her eyes. "Anyway, what happened with your father? Why does he hate you so much?"

"At first I thought it was because I get in trouble all the time. But I'm starting to believe it's something else. And I won't let him do to me what he did to Ace. He was my favorite brother. He cared about me. And I cared about him. But the moment he went against what father believed, he got rid of him and took away his money."

"We need to find out why he hates you so much. Who can you ask?"

"I don't know."

"Nobody in this family fucks with you?"

She thought harder. "Maybe I can get Spacey drunk. He talks when he's had a lot to drink." She wiped her tears. "Everybody knows–"

"What did you do to my dog?" Minnesota asked Sharon.

"Nothing...I was playing with him and–"

"I don't know what your obsession is with my animal but I'm going to need you to leave him alone."

She focused on her sister. "Now what's wrong with you?"

"You mean outside of you trying to be a mother to my daughter?"

"I'm not trying to be a mother. But I do wanna make sure she's good. And sometimes you act like it's not a problem and other times you do."

"What you talking about?"

"When you need a babysitter or you want me to watch her. But when you want to feel loved you want me to hand her over. Well, I'm not doing that anymore. Just so you know."

Blakeslee looked at her sister and took off running down the hallway. Her feet slapped against the corridor floor.

While her friend was in despair, Sharon looked at Pit-Pat as if he would jump out of Minnie's arms and into hers.

He didn't.

So she followed Blakeslee.

Blakeslee was almost in her room when she spotted Mason.

He grabbed her forearm. His warm touch caused her body to pulse. "What's going on, Blakeslee? Why you upset?"

"Father hates me! Minnesota hates me! My baby girl hates me! Do you know why?" Her eyes darted from him to the floor to the ceiling.

He wasn't certain about Minnesota and Sugar, but he had his ideas why Banks wasn't a fan. For starters she shared his dead name and Banks hated that about his daughter. He wasn't even the one who chose the name.

Jersey did.

Had she been any smarter and knew him more intimately she would have known it was a bad idea.

Unfortunately, she was long gone.

And Mason felt that if Banks had his way, Blakeslee would be gone too.

CHAPTER EIGHT
LIKE THE DADDY BUT DIFFERENT

Joey, Walid, and Mason sat in the pool house as smooth music boomed from the speakers embedded in the ceiling. The neon blue lights stemming from the pool floor caused wave-like patterns on their chocolate and light skin tones.

Every nigga present was dipped in diamonds.

Although Mason wanted to talk to them both about something important, he realized that as of right now Ace was an uncomfortable topic for all involved. Besides, he ruined their lives by causing problems and destroying their family bond.

It was difficult not having him around. And it was difficult knowing that he was somewhere with revenge in his heart.

Still, there was nothing that was going to stop Mason from stating his peace.

Or from loving his son.

At the same time, all needed to heed his warning.

"I want to talk to you both about something." Mason said as he sank in his chair, water drops bubbled on his velvet skin.

"I knew something was up." Joey said, shaking his head.

"Why you say that?"

"I haven't seen you in this pool house in years. If you're not in the lounge, you're at the beach. If you're not at the beach you sliding off to get in something wet."

Mason chuckled thinking about the last Belizean beauty he fucked a few weeks back.

"But you're never in this pool." Joey continued.

"I want to talk about Ace."

Walid shook his head. Although he was his own man whenever he got in trouble, he always felt some sort of responsibility when Ace was out there causing havoc. Mainly because he was his brother.

Twin brother at that.

So moving about the world causing issues at the same time didn't sit right with his spirit. The man literally had his face.

Although unlike Walid, Ace's face had already begun to show the signs of stress and age.

While Walid looked as smooth as untouched butter.

"I'm listening." Walid said.

"You both need to go get your sons."

Joey glared. "Hold up, did you say *our* sons? You brought me here for this meeting? When you know how I feel about that bitch!"

"I'm just saying."

"Sydney fucked my brother and then had a son by him." His nostrils flared. "So my blood does not cross through his veins. The only thing we have in common is our last name. So I'm with, pops on this situation. The nigga Ace is dead to me. And he needs to be dead to you too."

"He's my twin," Walid said in a low voice that was just stating the facts.

"You heard me right?" He pointed in his face.

Walid walked off, respecting the fact that Joey was on his big brother shit.

Mason was frustrated so he tried to take a different approach.

"By now the obvious is clear. My last name is Louisville. Your last name is Wales. But this family has merged. And I care about both sides deeply. Roman Wales is a member of this family. And if Ace is no longer in Mexico, we need to get ahead of that ASAP. Starting with the protection of Baltimore and Roman before he manages to get to them."

Joey stormed to the short table next to his pool chair, grabbed his glass and drank what was left. Snatching the towel off the rack, he dried his face and his diamond necklace. "I love you, Uncle Mason. But I don't want nothing to do with that boy." He stormed out.

Mason's chin lowered to his chest. He figured he would react that way but was hoping that he would try and be reasonable also.

"Sorry, pops." Walid said.

"It's not your fault, son." He rubbed his eyes.

"But don't be too hard on Joey though. I was there when he got the news that Ace slept with Sydney and got her pregnant."

"I didn't know that."

"It was crazy. I was sitting outside of their house in the car praying he wouldn't kill her. The pain he felt was heavy. All in his eyes."

"I get all that. But he needs to be reminded that this family sticks together no matter what."

"I think it's wrong to ask him to take care of another man's seed."

"I have to go back to what we stand for as a combined family. It's not only another man's seed. The boy is a Wales. The boy is your nephew. The boy is our blood." He took a deep breath.

Walid nodded.

"What you plan to do about Baltimore?"

Walid nodded. "I'm not going to lie; this got me uneasy. But I trust father. I trust you too. In my heart I feel like Ace is not a problem."

He was looking downward as he paced the pool house floor. It was like he was trying to convince himself about the danger that was looming.

"Nicolas, from what I understood, was a common criminal." Walid continued. "To be honest, I just want us to move on with our lives."

"Okay, I hear you. So do me this solid. Since my blood courses through your veins."

"Anything."

"I know you're not going to take your son away and bring him back here. You've made your position clear in the past, although I told you how I feel about my grandson being in the States. But just go check on them. I want to know that they okay. And if you detect anything despite the promise you made to Aliyah, bring Roman and Baltimore back."

Walid resonated with the request and said, "I'll see what I can do."

A porno played on a television as Ace sat in the living room of the brothel house.

The smell of raw sex, cheap perfume and over fried chicken wings wafted into the air.

The ladies kept the porno channel on to keep their clients in the mood at all times.

But he was watching something else.

Reality TV if you will.

From where his recliner was posted he could see inside of a room through the cracked door. An oversized man was lying on his back while the prostitute sat with her hairy pussy over his lips. She was giving him a sloppy blow job 69 style.

Every so often she would look up and see Ace staring.

He didn't smile.

He didn't make a move.

He just looked at them both.

And for some reason she enjoyed his gaze.

Her name was Keke.

And she was a beautiful snake.

Closing her red silk robe from upstairs, Arbella walked toward him. Her bare feet slid across the hardwood floors. "What did you do to your hair? Why do you have blond streaks?"

"I wanna change shit up."

She nodded. "Okay...what is your plan for Walid and Banks?"

"I don't have to do anything."

She felt like he was lying. "I don't get it."

"By now they would have found out I'm not in Mexico. And if I know my father, he'll be pretending like it doesn't matter. Like I can't lay hands on a nigga." He shifted his dick just cause. "But he is worried." His brows lowered. "He is concerned." He smiled sinisterly. "And he should be."

"And then?"

Silence.

"Ace, talk to me!"

When she followed his gaze and saw Keke giving head while looking at her nigga, she grew angry. "I'm no longer comfortable here. We need to get out of this house. I know they've agreed to give you money, but I think we can get funds another way. So when can we—"

Slowly his eyes moved up toward her, stopping her sentence. "We will leave when I get ready. And not a moment sooner."

"Why do I feel like I'm a second thought? Why do I feel like you don't care about me the same anymore?"

If ever he loved a female, she was it.

It was important to let her know nobody could take her place.

So, he grabbed her hand gently and pulled her down. She positioned herself on his lap. "If I told you the things that were done to me in Mexico you wouldn't believe them. And I don't need anybody feeling pity for me, so I won't go into detail. I just want you to understand in order for me to love you how I want to love you, I have to deal with this issue first. If not, I promise you, we will not have the life we deserve. My mind won't be with you. My dick won't move for you. Is that what you desire?"

CHAPTER NINE
SLITHER

As Mason sat in his office with his assistant making several calls, he couldn't get over the fear that his son was on his way to cause problems.

The worst part about it all was that he appeared to be alone in his plight. No one else seemed to care about the danger looming around.

If he wanted to prevent devastation he would have to put in the work himself.

And so, he spent the next day or so trying to find anybody who would know Ace's whereabouts. He even hired a crew in Mexico to knock on doors.

He spared no expense.

Some of the leads ended in vain and others did provide a little light.

For instance, he discovered that Ace did in fact live with Nicolas. It unfolded that they both committed crimes together throughout Mexico which entailed robbery, burglary and even murder. Most people indicated that if Ace wasn't Nicolas' son, he sure acted like he was.

None of this made sense to Mason. Nicolas was not an appealing man. He possessed dark energy and hate wherever he went.

And yet Ace found a home in his company?

What the fuck?

Frustrated and confused upon learning more, Mason flopped on the sofa and his assistant quickly grabbed him a glass of whiskey.

Vanessa may have been on payroll, but she aspired for bigger things. She saw how well they took care of the people surrounding their island. But more than it all, how lavish the lifestyle was of the women who entered a Wales or Louisville bed.

Then she heard tale of Walid making a native woman his girl and having a child with her.

She wanted the same fairytale.

Vanessa couldn't get over the fact that Banks and Mason were as old as they were. Both had looks as if they were in their early 40's and the money made them forever young.

If she was going to get into this family, she had to find a way. And so she focused all of her attention on what Mason wasn't saying. On what he needed. After some time she noticed a deep loneliness.

And she hoped she could correct that by first helping his plight, to find Ace, so she could eventually be his wife.

"I was able to get in contact with a younger girl. About 14-years-old in Mexico." She was holding a stack of papers in her hand which included many handwritten notes.

Mason sat the glass on the table and gave her his undivided attention. "Go on."

"She seemed to believe that Ace is no longer in Mexico. She mentioned something about him catching a flight but she wasn't sure."

The hairs on Mason skin rose slightly. And he could tell she possessed more information than she let on. "You know something else. You're holding back. What is it?"

"I really don't wanna say it, but the island girl is known for lying."

He picked his glass of whiskey back up. "What am I gonna do with that shit? There is no way that I can take the word of a liar. I need concrete evidence that my son is no longer in Mexico. Why would you even bring this to me? When you know how serious this is."

"I'm not as smart as you are. And I understand I could come across as naïve at times. But I'm telling you

I believe this girl. You should really look deeper into it, Mason. She even sounded scared to tell me."

Mason was so anxious his lungs felt as if they wouldn't expand. He kept breathing deeply and exhaling. Despite doing that several times that day he still couldn't seem to get his body comfortable.

Relaxed.

"You look stressed."

Seeing this she dropped to her knees and removed his shoes. The smell of the new leathers from his designer sandals rushed into her nose. She started with his left foot and then his right.

Massaging it fully it didn't take long for him to relax and within very little time he melted under her touch.

He wasn't dumb.

She wanted more.

Shit was out of order and he didn't need another problem.

"I know what you want." He said firmly. "And I will never give you the life you desire."

She stopped massaging his foot. "What are you talking about?"

"You and I both know."

When he saw Banks walk by his office he yelled, "Banks! Come here!"

Banks was in a hurry because he and Faye were on their next schedule for an upcoming business. So, the last thing he wanted was to be wasting time on him and his theories about Ace.

He walked to his doorway. "What is it?" He stared at the assistant who always seemed to be doing everything but work in his opinion.

Knowing that he didn't like her and also being fully aware who had the most power in the mansion, Vanessa hustled out so as to not irritate the boss.

Banks entered. "I've never seen an assistant massage feet before. But then again you've always been an irregular sort of guy."

"We have to talk."

Banks shook his head. "I've already stated my piece as it relates to our son. So I'm going to need you to leave the matter alone."

"You don't even know what I'm gonna talk about and you're already making excuses."

He smiled, wanting to catch him in a lie. "So this isn't about Ace?"

It actually was but he didn't want to give him the satisfaction. The look on his face was enough to make his stomach turn. It would have to wait until later.

"No. What's going on with you in Blakeslee?"

He was fighting mad.

He didn't feel like talking about her at all.

"That girl is a troublemaker. Whenever I look at her she reminds me of Ace. If things continue as they are she's going to have to find her own place on the island."

Mason couldn't believe his ears. "Since I have known you, you've always done your best to take care of every member of this family. Even those who don't share your direct bloodline. Me included."

"What you getting at? Because I'm already aware of my charities."

The nigga was mad cocky.

"It was a goal of yours to keep everybody in the same house. But over these past couple of years the hate you've had for Ace and Blakeslee is gross. And it's unlike the man I knew who wanted to be a protector."

"Well, maybe you don't know anything about me after all."

Mason chuckled. "My nigga, I'm the only one who knows *everything* about you. I know you better than your wife. Tell me it's not true. I'll wait."

He looked down.

Point proved.

"So answer me...why do you hate that girl so much?" Mason continued. "What else could she have possibly done to make you look at her the way that you do?"

"You always want a story. But some things just are."

"The way you treat your children and the hate you have for them will come back on you. And I'm trying to prevent that Karma."

"You don't know what you're talking about."

"Be careful with Blakeslee. She needs you to see her. Like you see everyone else. That's all I'm asking you to do. As a brother."

He laughed. "And if I don't, *brother*? What will become of us?"

Mason shook his head and grabbed his whiskey. Standing up he glared at him once more, east Baltimore style. "You been feelin' yourself lately. But I'll let you have it. For now." He bopped out the door.

CHAPTER TEN
BROKEN SUGAR

Minnesota was sitting on the massive deck behind the mansion with Sugar on her lap. Pit-Pat ran on the deck happily while playing with his favorite thing. A large strawberry shaped chew toy.

The breeze caused strands of their hair to dance, twerk and spin.

It had yet to rain.

As she looked down, she could no longer express the amount of love that she had for her niece. And although it should have trailed along the lines of her being an aunt, it went much deeper.

She did feel like she was her mother.

She adored this little girl.

It wasn't just Minnesota who loved Sugar.

It was as if she could sense who in the family needed love the most and she would direct her little attention toward the person.

It was giving big adult energy.

Whenever someone had a bad day, her small feet would go slapping towards the person and before you knew it her arms would be extended upward as she would beg to be held.

At first it would seem as if she needed a hug. But it was obvious after some time that the adult was the one who was relieved upon her touch.

Some people believe one of the other reasons Minnesota gravitated toward Sugar was because it was whispered that she could not have children of her own. Every baby that entered her womb was not brought to full term. So she was resigned to the fact that it would never happen.

That she was barren.

She was still enjoying Sugar's company when her sister entered the picture. "I came to get my baby." Blakeslee hung in the doorway of the mansion.

This bitch.

Minnesota looked at her and then focused back on Sugar who was reading a book in her lap. "Not right now."

She glared. "Yes, now! This is my daughter. I mean you're getting kind of weird with it. Like you have rights to her or something. Even got father believing it! We didn't have this child together you know. You ain't the father, girl."

Minnesota rubbed the back of her neck to prevent going off.

Because everyone in the house knew that Blakeslee had no control or say so when it came to Sugar. In the beginning it was because she appeared to not want to be a mother.

But after some time, people just didn't trust her with the golden child.

When they gave in, Sugar would be left with Blakeslee and she would have a bruise afterwards. Or days would go by and her pamper wouldn't be changed. Then there were the times when she would straight up forget to feed the baby.

But since Sugar was a family favorite, everyone was highly protective.

"I know what you want me to do, Blakeslee. If I were you I would just leave it alone."

"I don't know what you're talking about."

"Except you do. You want this baby to fear me."

"You sound stupid."

"Don't get yourself hurt, Blakeslee. You haven't known this family as long as I've known this family. We are very overprotective of those we care about. And we love this little girl too much to let you harm her."

"I didn't know this family as long as you?" She giggled. "You act like I'm adopted or something. My blood courses through father's veins. Through hers too." She pointed at the baby.

"I love you," Sugar said to Minnesota. She then turned to her mother and said, "I love you too. Be nice, mama."

"Don't talk back to me!" Blakeslee yelled.

"Blakeslee, go in the house!" Minnie yelled. "We don't want you out here."

Blakeslee, still hurt that Banks appeared to not want to have anything to do with her, stormed off the patio. And with rage not necessary she pulled Sugar by her arm and it snapped.

Minnesota lost it.

Pit-Pat ran into the house.

Seeing her niece in so much pain caused her blood to boil.

Sugar screaming, coupled with the dumb look on Blakeslee's face made her snap. Had she had her weapon she would have taken her down.

For now, she snatched Sugar out of her arms and placed her carefully on the chair. Then she hit her with a left to the face followed by a right. Blakeslee wasn't a fighter, so she was shocked to be the recipient of so many of her big sister's blows.

But Minnesota was focused and continued to pound away.

It was mayhem!

Mason, hearing the commotion, rushed out to the balcony just as Banks followed him.

"What's going on!" Mason yelled, pulling her off Blakeslee whose light skin was bruised. He grabbed both of Minnesota's wrists. "Stop!"

"She broke her arm!" Minnesota said. "She broke her fucking arm!"

Banks, who just came out, was so angry he stood in front of it all, as stiff as a statue.

Mason's jaw dropped upon hearing the news. "What you mean she broke her arm?"

"It was an accident!" Blakeslee yelled, feeling her world closing in. "Please don't be angry with me."

Spacey, also hearing the noise, ran out just in time. "What's going on?"

He looked at Sugar who was whimpering but quite honestly handling the pain like a G.

Dare we say...like a Wales.

"Blakeslee broke Sugar's arm!" Minnesota yelled.

"This bitch stupid," Spacey said after assessing quickly what happened. "Just like the nigga Ace. Always causing issues for our family." He lifted Sugar off the chair and rushed her into the house.

Mason released Minnesota and she followed closely behind him.

When they were gone Banks stood in front of Blakeslee who was trembling. "I'm sick of you. And I want you out of this house."

"Banks, find out what's going on first before you cut her off." Mason said.

"It was an accident!" She cried to Banks. "I promise it was an accident!"

"So you're not sorry you hurt your own daughter?" He asked.

"I didn't mean–."

Just as quickly as everything began, with a closed fist, Banks stole her in the face. Blood gushed everywhere from her nose and lips.

He didn't care.

He was about to strike her again until Mason rushed up behind him and grabbed his fist. "I love you, brother. But you won't do that in front of me. Not again." His breath was heavy and sure.

Sharon was right.

Mason did come to the rescue.

Banks looked back at him, at her, and snatched away before storming inside the house.

Helping Blakeslee off the ground, he picked her up and walked her into the house and down the hallway. Once in her room he took a towel from the rack the maid left for going to the beach and pool. Dampening the edge in her sink, he returned to the bedroom where she lay on the mattress.

Slowly he dabbed her split lips to clean up the blood. The towel turned a soft pink with each press. As he continued to clean up the wound she wept.

He felt sorry for her.

He knew what it meant to be an outcast.

Unlike so many other members of the family he didn't think she was vicious on purpose. He believed she was ignored. He believed she was overlooked. And so his heart poured out to her in ways others couldn't understand.

"He wants me to be a monster. Doesn't he?" She cried. "If he will, I would gladly oblige."

"Stop talking wild."

"It's true."

"There are some things that are going on with your father that I don't feel comfortable expressing to you. And I'm sorry because I know you're in a lot of pain."

"Why do you take up for him so much?"

"There's not enough time in the day for me to tell you why I take up for him. And to be honest, what's understood between Banks and I doesn't have to be explained. To anyone. But I will say this is the worst I've ever seen him. So don't take it personally. Please. Something else is going on."

She continued to cry and as he sat on the edge of the bed, suddenly she laid her head in his lap while he wiped her soft black hair with his hands.

He looked down and then away because every time he saw her face he was taken back to the past.

A past that always haunted him.

When Blakeslee was a young girl she looked so much like Banks it gave him chills. He watched her turn from a child to a beautiful woman so troubled, he thought she would run away to escape it all.

And yet Mason knew more troubled him.

There was no doubt that if Banks would have remained female, he would look exactly like the young woman in his lap. A young woman who was now an adult that he was having trouble not being attracted to.

"Thank you for loving me." She said, gripping his legs as her face remained in his lap.

"Stop talking wild. You my niece."

If she turned her head just an inch, her face would be in his crotch which was thickening more every second.

"Thank you for not treating me like the devil. Thank you for always coming to my rescue. I truly don't know what I would do without you and I'm so glad you are here, Mason."

And then she did it.

When she turned her head as if she was going to inhale him down below, he jumped up and rushed out the room.

"I'm sorry. I just have to go." He said leaving her alone.

Later on that night...

Blakeslee and Sharon were sharing drinks with Spacey in the living room. They poured him more shots than he could consume.

Because there was no way Blakeslee would go another day without finding out more about Mason and Banks' past.

Now it was time for seduction.

And for a Wales, there was no greater topic than himself. And so, they asked Spacey about life in Baltimore. They asked him about how fly he was in the city.

Sharon even made it her business to sit on his lap and twerk, which caused him to focus on his senses instead of the thoughts and words exiting his mind.

Sure, her locs stank every now and again.

She was still pretty.

With time, Spacey, due to the liquor and the attention, gave them just what they needed.

Answers.

The keys to why Mason was so enthralled with Blakeslee.

With a glass of Mason and Joey's tequila in hand he said, "He fucks with you because you look just like pops did. When he was a little girl. And say what you want..." He pointed at her with the glass. "...pops loves Faye, but he will always love Mason more."

Blakeslee and Sharon smiled.

Now she knew her next move.

CHAPTER ELEVEN
SEDUCE, BITCH!

Ace, Aliyah, and Arbella sat in the backyard at the brothel. Despite it being a weekend, it was relatively quiet inside.

Normally for such a nice night the house would be bustling with men looking to be fucked. But that wasn't the case tonight.

And he preferred it that way.

"He hasn't answered any of my calls." Aliyah said. "I mean if it's about our son he does respond. Other than that, he doesn't answer me if I ask basic questions. So I don't know what he's thinking."

"When you spoke to him last, what did he say?"

"He asked me if Baltimore was fine and when I said he was he hung up."

"Tell me from the start why you broke up with him?"

"Ace, I can't think of an answer to all these questions right now. Between Sydney asking me what's going on with Roman and me losing my mind over not having Baltimore home..." She looked down and back at him.

"...I mean, can I at least lay eyes on him? I'm begging you."

He looked up at Arbella and nodded.

She walked away leaving them alone.

"I'm giving you what you need, by seeing Baltimore, so you can give me what I want. But you have to understand I'm no longer the man I used to be. I'm not the boy you met in Belize. Things are different with me these days. So I'm going to need you to start answering my questions. Otherwise, you'll be of no use to me. And I'll have to hurt you. And my nephew."

"Please don't..." She shook her head rapidly. "I'll do whatever you want."

"Now...tell me again why he broke up with you."

"It was because of what you said. The part about him being responsible for my father being killed in that accident. Remember, you told me that. And I told him."

"If you're blaming this on me it won't work. Anyway, in my mind that would never have been enough for my brother to leave you. So what else happened?"

She took a deep pull. "I left him."

"That makes more sense."

She dragged both hands and wiped them down her face. "But I need to be clear, no matter who left who, he's done with me. Trust me. I tried everything."

"We have the same DNA. I know what needs to happen to get him back. But you're gonna have to change everything about yourself."

When Arbella walked in with her son, who was happy, clean, and healthy, Aliyah smiled. He was even wearing new tennis shoes and a shirt.

"Thank you for getting him new clothing," Aliyah said.

"He's still my nephew. He gotta stay fresh. Let's just hope I won't make it bloody."

"Ace!"

He grinned.

"Uh...I...where is Roman?" Aliyah trembled while hugging her son.

"Hold up...you asked to see your son and here he is. Don't worry about mine."

After she was sure her son was okay, Arbella took him back upstairs. It wasn't easy pulling him from her arms, but Arbella made it happen.

"Okay now you laid eyes on nephew. Finish talking. When he came over in the past, what have you done to get his attention?"

She scratched her scalp. "To be honest I haven't done anything effectively. I bring up being with him from time-to-time, but he always manages to bring it back to Baltimore."

Ace shook his head. "You think I'm asking basic questions. And I'm not. And your refusal to answer me exactly how I want is getting on my fucking nerves. Making my dick soft. So again I want to know the specifics."

"We talked about childcare. The stipend that's set up for him. Things that don't really need to be spoken about, but I use it as an opportunity to keep dialogue flowing between us. And nothing I do seems to work. Trust me. There is nothing more I want then to get back with him, but he's simply not interested."

He believed her.

"A couple months back I made dinner. His favorite. Asked if he wanted to eat with me and he laughed and walked out the door. I knew then he was done for sure."

"Have you offered him up sexually?"

"There's no way possible I would do something like that."

"Why not?"

"I don't know."

"I think you do know."

She looked down at her hands and back at him. "I don't want to be rejected. It hurts too much."

"Go nasty." He pointed at him. "Be aggressive with him. He wants to feel like you really are wanting him. So the things you used to do back in the day that made him come running to you won't work anymore. You have to make clear that you want my brother again. Act as if life depends on it. Because it does."

CHAPTER TWELVE
SANDSTORMS

Mason was fuming.

After seeing how Banks handled Blakeslee a few days ago, he still couldn't get out of his own head. He wasn't sure what happened or what was going on with his friend, but he knew he was changing, and it appeared to be for the worst.

Storming back and forth along the beach, causing sand clouds to fly everywhere he tried to calm himself down. Because if things continued as they were, he was certain that a fight would break out between them.

And that someone would get hurt, greatly.

He was just getting ready to go back in the house and grab a glass when the man who was on his mind stormed out on the beach. His white button-down linen shirt flowed in the wind. And his trademark gait was overly exaggerated due to being angry.

A half million dollars alone rested on their necks, wrists, and fingers.

"We have to talk!" Banks yelled.

He was literally the last person on earth he wanted to see. "I suggest you leave me alone at this moment!"

"Hold up, you threatening me?"

"I said what needed to be said. You really don't want to talk to me right now." He paced in front of him like a lion. "Because I watched you take a closed fist to your daughter's face. And I'm not feeling the shit."

"You still talking about that shit?"

Silence.

"So you're going to say nothing about her breaking Sugar's arm?" Banks continued.

"Yes I'm going to say something about that."

"Did you say anything about it?"

"It happened all so quick."

He moved closer. "It's quite simple. Did you say something to Blakeslee for breaking her own daughter's arm or not?"

"We did have a conversation about it. And she was upset about how everything went down. And to be honest I believe her."

"You can play games with her if you want. But I need you to understand something. I see the same thing in her I saw in Ace. Manipulation. Jealousy. And I don't want that for our family. So if you have a problem with-"

"Instead of talking to her you got violent. Hit her in the face! What if you would have killed her? We grown ass men! The way you went about all this shit is foul."

Banks suddenly grew uncomfortable. "What is it with you and her? Why do you feel the need to rescue her so much? Why do you feel the need to rescue Ace so much? It's almost as if you're working against this family. It's giving treason."

Mason stepped closer. "Treason! What the fuck you trying to imply?"

He pointed at the ground. "I'm asking a specific question. And I still haven't gotten an answer. What is it with you and my daughter?"

"So she's your daughter now? Because just a minute ago she was a nigga on the street! I mean…maybe you should make up your mind." He chuckled.

"You letting her get in your head." He gave direct probing eye contact. "I suggest you be careful. Because no matter what you do, she will never be me." He chuckled lightly.

"Fuck is that supposed to mean?"

"Fake dumb if you want to, but we both know what it is." He floated away.

CHAPTER THIRTEEN
THANKS FOR MY CHILD

Sydney kept circling the space in front of Aliyah's bedroom door.

Her arms were crossed tightly over her chest and she was waiting for her to leave the bathroom before she knocked. She had so many questions that played in her mind and she felt as if she were about to explode.

Unfortunately she was unable to wait.

Using all her strength she banged on the door with a closed fist until Aliyah appeared on the other side. It was obvious she had been crying too.

"Not now." She walked around her and towards the kitchen.

"What do you mean not now?" She wiped her tears. "What is he doing with my baby? I don't have nothing to do with this shit! Joey doesn't even claim our son!"

"Do you at least hear yourself? You're coming at me like I'm the one in charge of all this. I told you before that I'm doing the best to get both of our sons back. And whether you like it or not you're going to have to trust and believe me."

115

"Well what does he want? You have to at least know that. Because I'm the mother and he won't even answer my calls!"

Aliyah moved to the refrigerator and grabbed a box of wine. "I honestly don't know what he wants. The only plan that appears to be in motion now is that he wants me to speak to Walid."

"Does he miss him or something?"

Aliyah sighed deeply. "Sydney, I know you're upset. But my head is throbbing. Just like your baby is in his possession, mine is too. And I'm not about to let you throw me off my game."

A fake smile sat on her face. "I should've never allowed you to move in with me."

Aliyah glared. "What you just say?"

"I should have known your Belizean ass was trouble from the get-go." Her skin flushed red.

"You're playing right?"

"I'm not playing! You have been jealous of me from the moment you laid eyes on me."

"Sydney, I don't wanna go off on you. I swear I don't. So let me make this clear. There is nothing about you that I would ever be jealous of. Your husband doesn't even want you. We are not the same."

"Explain."

116

"I gave up my relationship with Walid because I was hurt about what he did to my father. That makes us different. But what do you go do? Sleep with his brother. So when I tell you there's nothing about you that makes me want your life please believe me."

Her lips clenched together. "I want my son back. And I will cause all kinds of problems until that happens." She stepped closer. "What is that saying niggas love?"

It was giving racism so she was afraid. "Be easy, girl."

"I just don't give a fuck no more!" She ran off.

Aliyah sat on her sofa with the window open.

Ace was on her right and Arbella was on her left. The sky was dark gray and it was obvious that a storm was coming at any time.

The cell phone sat in her lap and trembled like she did. If she wasn't careful it would fall on the floor and shatter into a million pieces.

"When you call him this time, you have to be calm." Ace said in a low soothing voice.

"I'm trying. I swear to God I am."

"Think about what's at stake. That should help you enough."

"What is at stake?" She tossed her arms up. "Maybe if I knew more details that would help me."

"The only thing you need to realize at this point is that I have your son. If that's not enough motivation, I don't know what to tell you."

Tears fell down her cheeks. "I don't get it." She whispered. "I've been trying to see things the way you want me to see them and I just can't."

"The reason he was in the kind of pain he was in when you left him was because he adored you. And I'm pretty sure if you can play the tapes back in your mind he probably begged you not to leave him."

He did.

"But you did anyway right? And so that's the last thing he was stuck with. Men have feelings too. Especially when they want a woman enough to take them from their own brother." He glared while briefly remembering when she belonged to him as a teenager. "He will come back but he needs to feel safe first."

"What if he has a girlfriend?"

"If I know my brother he has lots of bitches. But there's only one of you."

"You're not your brother!" Arbella yelled. "I mean how can you be so sure? You talk as if you were the man himself."

He loved her so much but since she had lost her father and her lifestyle, she seemed to be cynical. His plan was to build her up once things worked out as he envisioned.

For now, he had to keep her in her place.

"Do you want me to say something to hurt your feelings? If you do, you need to know if I go there I'm not gonna waste any time building you back up when you're destroyed. So do you want to take a seat or do you want me to rage on you?"

Arbella took her seat.

He focused back on Aliyah. "Make the call. I have plans. And my plans aren't moving quickly enough for me."

Raising the phone in her lap she hit the icon which held his number.

"Breathe." Ace directed as if she was an actress in a movie.

It wasn't until that moment that she realized she wasn't breathing. And so she took a deep breath just as Walid answered the phone. "Everything ok with Baltimore?"

"Uh…yes."

"Well I'm glad you called."

Her eyes lit up. "Really, Walid?"

Ace and Arbella leaned in due to her excitement.

"Why are you glad?" She questioned softly.

"Because I plan on coming out there tomorrow."

"That's…that's great."

"Hold up, why do you sound excited?"

"I just wasn't expecting you until next month."

"Yeah I guess I'm feeling like seeing my boy. Where is he? Let me talk to him."

"He's with some friends on a playdate. Do you want me to go get him?"

"No, let him have fun. I'll spend time with him when I get there."

"Ok. See you then."

"I'll let you know when I'm closer."

"Give him more," Ace whispered in the background.

Aliyah looked over at Arbella who was glaring her way.

If Arbella didn't hate her so much Aliyah would feel comfortable relying on her for moral support. But she could tell that she wanted her out of the picture just as much as she wanted to be gone.

So if she was going to do this, if she was going to seduce Walid, it would have to be on her own.

"I guess I'll wait for you to come back. I know Baltimore will be excited."

"Aliyah…"

"Yes, Walid."

"You seen my brother 'round there?"

She farted and looked over at him. He was right in her face. "No…I haven't."

"Well why did you call?"

"I guess I wanted to hear your voice."

Ace smiled.

Walid hung up.

Aliyah looked at Ace. "You got him."

"How did you get that from that? He fucking hung up."

"He's triggered. It's all in his voice."

CHAPTER FOURTEEN
I CAN'T WAIT TO BE KING

Riot was in the home gym with Patrick and Bolt lifting weights.

Patrick and Bolt were taking longer on their side then he believed they should and so he grew irritated.

Lately they seemed to take advantage of Riot and pushed him over and so he hoped getting fit would gain their respect. In their minds he was soft. So he wanted to be strong, hoping they would accept him.

It never happened.

"So, what's up with that stupid ass girlfriend of yours?" Patrick yelled out of the blue.

Riot wanted to shit himself.

Bolt, on the other hand, broke out laughing.

"My girl not dumb."

"Are you serious? I told her the other day that Banks makes water for the ocean and she believed me."

He and Bolt laughed harder.

"She's smarter than you think."

"Yeah, aight."

"You know what, it's my turn to get on the weights." Riot made an announcement.

"Wait a minute!" Patrick said, wiping the sweat off his brow with his T-shirt even though towels waited for him on the rack by the door. "It ain't like you gonna lift heavy anyway. With them weak ass arms."

Riot was growing angrier.

So he walked over to them and grabbed the dumbbells. They were right. His arms were weak, and the weights were heavy, so he almost pulled his arm out of the socket, but he didn't care. At least Patrick couldn't use them at the moment.

Slowly Patrick sat up on the bench and looked over at him.

Bolt hung to his left.

"Fuck you do that for?" Patrick yelled.

"I told you it was my turn and y'all didn't listen. Do you hear me now?" He was hoping to be as Wales as possible.

Firm.

Sure.

Patrick and Bolt laughed harder which was angering Riot to no end.

"You know what, get out of my gym." Riot responded. "I'm sick of looking at y'all."

Patrick stopped laughing. "This isn't your gym. This is *our* gym."

"Is it though? Because my grandfather made it clear that I'm going to inherit his money and his land. So basically, when he dies, I'm going to own all this shit anyway. That means I make the rules."

"Boy, if you don't sit your lower-class ass down!" Patrick continued.

"Low class! I'm a billionaire's grandson! You just a nigga from Baltimore."

"You know what, what if we don't leave?" Patrick said, walking closely to him. "What you going to do then?"

Riot thought hard about the question.

To be honest he hadn't even planned on saying what he did. But after learning that he was really an heir, he felt it was time for him to be proper cocky.

"Then I'll tell my grandfather to put you out."

Patrick laughed softly although he was definitely scared now.

While Bolt looked as if he wanted to piss on himself.

"Uncle Banks is not going to throw us out because you say something. You feeling yourself now for real."

"I mean do you really want to try me?"

"Maybe we should let him use the weights." Bolt said, legit scared. "I'm done anyway."

Patrick wanted to steal him in the jaw but instead stared at him intensely. "Yeah I'm done too. Stinks in here anyway."

Walking down the hallway Patrick looked over at Bolt and whispered, "Don't you got his girlfriend's number?"

"Yep. Why?"

"Tell her to come over here. I want to say a few things in her ear."

Bolt laughed. "I like the sound of that shit already."

Sharon sat on the bed next to Blakeslee who was trying to cover her bruised face with make-up.

Banks hitting her days back forced her heart to pump rage. She had some plans that she wanted to see through and she felt she needed to look the part.

"So I got the backstory from Spacey but tell me again how Mason is not related to you."

She giggled. "Mason is my father's friend. They grew up together or some shit like that. But that doesn't make us related."

"Ok, why does everybody call him Uncle Mason then?"

"Only my father's children, except for Ace and Walid, call him Uncle Mason. I never really liked the name. And I'm glad I didn't use it that much when everyone else did. Because if I had, my plan wouldn't work."

"What are you going to do again?"

"I wanna see if what Spacey said was true. Does he think I'm father as a girl? From back when they were kids. In middle or high school." Her eyes lit up.

Sharon rubbed her hands together. "I like the sound of this, I swear to God."

"To be honest I'm not sure what I will do if he wants me that way. When we were together when I was hit in the face by father, I felt like he was pulling back from me. So if I put the pressure on him a little more, and then you put that spell on him, then maybe he will see things my way."

"What do you want with him when you get him?"

"Power. To use him to get back at father. To tear them a part."

She nodded. "Smart. Real smart." She took a deep breath. "But this time I don't want money for the spell."

She frowned. "What do you want?"

"I want the dog."

"Why do you have an obsession with that mothafucka? It's getting weird for real for real."

"Oh, so you get to be obsessed but I don't?"

"My sister will never part with that bitch."

"You better make it happen. Because the spell you're asking me about really needs my intentions involved. And I'm not gonna really be with it if I'm not feeling like there's something in it for me too."

"You make Mason fall in love with me then I'll get you anything you want. Even a fat ass French bulldog that shits on your lap."

The two women laughed softly.

Mason was brushing his hair in his bathroom.

After he was done, he cleared his nose and threw it in the trash. Once dressed he left his room to meet up with a Belizean cutie who had his attention.

The moment he was gone Sharon took hair from his brush and the soiled tissue paper, before leaving out.

CHAPTER FIFTEEN
SNEAKY LINK

Minnesota stood in the doorway of Sugar's bedroom and looked at her lovingly as she lay in her bed. On the floor, Pit-Pat looked at the child too, having sensed Sugar was injured.

Despite having her arm broken, the little girl was a trooper. And she still managed to exude love while in pain. So, it did Minnesota's heart good to see her getting some much-needed rest.

"How is she?" Banks asked, looking intently at his granddaughter sleeping. The man exuded strength even when he wasn't trying.

"She's fine, dad. They were able to give her a little something so that she wouldn't be in so much pain."

"I hope not too many drugs. We don't need her addicted like Joey when–"

"Of course not. I wouldn't let them."

He nodded. "I know. You're protective like me."

She could see sadness in his eyes. "What is it?"

He folded his hands in front of him." I don't understand Blakeslee. It's like her and Ace came from the same way of thinking. What could make them so jealous and vengeful?"

Minnesota took her father softly by the hand and closed the bedroom door. They stood in the corridor looking at one another.

Pit-Pat ran down the hallway barking all the way.

"That is a bad ass dog," he said.

She giggled. "Nah...he just happy."

He shook his head.

"Father, I appreciate what you did for Sugar when you came to her rescue. I could tell by the look in your eyes that you almost had a heart attack when you saw her little arm hanging loosely. But the way you hit Blakeslee was harsh."

"As far as I remember you hit her too."

"Yes. But she's my sister. I can do that."

He crossed his arms over his body. "I did react quickly. But I'm concerned."

"Concerned about what?"

"That she's going to cause the trouble that Ace did for our family. When he rejected us, I went back to the States because I thought I could bring him into our fold. And for a moment it caused me freedom. I won't let it happen again with her."

"Is that why you act like you don't have time for family lately?"

"Minnie."

"Father, I really wanna know. Because it sounds like you already have a plan for Blakeslee."

"I have some ideas. And not everyone may like it but at this point I can't take any more risks."

"What about Ace?"

"We good." He kissed her on her forehead and walked away.

When they went their separate ways they didn't check their surroundings.

The house was massive, and it was easy to lurk in the hallways and not be seen. But if they had checked they would've noticed that Blakeslee was hiding around the corner after having heard it all.

Could it be that Banks was really going to throw her out?

Rushing to her room she grabbed her cell phone. Sharon was inside playing with Minnesota's dog.

"What's up with you? And why you so happy?" Sharon questioned.

"I'm not sure but I got an idea."

"What?"

"If my favorite brother is home, I know who he may link up with." She hit one button on her cell and made a call. It rang a few times. "Julie, do you remember where my sister-in-law Sydney lives?"

"Who this?"

"Girl, don't play with me!"

"Oh, Blakeslee. I think I remember. She lives in the same neighborhood my rich aunt does. Why?"

"I'm gonna send some money to you. And I need you to have somebody sit on that house."

"Ok, who am I looking for?"

"You'll know him when you see him." She grinned. "Trust me."

CHAPTER SIXTEEN
SEXY PJ'S

Aliyah stood outside of Baltimore's room and watched him play by himself.

It felt good to have him home for the moment and at the same time she realized nothing was concrete if she didn't convince Walid to take her back.

She asked Ace millions of times what he wanted with their relationship, and he would never say anything other than make him fall in love again. So that's what she intended on trying to do in order to be reunited with her baby once and for all.

But then there was Sydney.

Down the hall she could hear her sniffling and crying. Ever since Ace maintained hold of his son Roman, she was experiencing a downward spiral.

Not to mention their friendship was done. They walked around the house as if they didn't know one another.

Barely speaking.

It was so bad that when the fire alarm went off in their home the other day Sydney walked out and stood in the front yard smoking a cigarette. She didn't even alert Aliyah that something may be wrong.

It turned out it was a malfunction on the smoke detector. But Aliyah couldn't get over the fact that she believed she wished for her death.

When the doorbell rang Aliyah rushed toward it before the sound awoke Sydney.

She saw her take two pills and figured she'd be out for the rest of the night. That would be enough time for her to try and make Walid see her again.

At least she hoped.

The moment she opened the door, and saw him standing before her, her knees grew weak. This wasn't a new thing. He always seemed to look better and better with time, and she wondered who was taking care of him.

Who was loving him?

Because it was obvious somebody was.

"Hi." She said, waving.

He looked at her clothing.

She started to wear a tight black spaghetti string dress to turn him on. But Ace said she had to look effortless in her beauty and sexuality. And so she chose a peach short pajama set two sizes too small. It cut into all areas of her body and her long hair dripped down her back and the sides of her face.

To bring shit home, she also rubbed a little oil on her skin that smelled of fresh fruit. Even in playing down her beauty she looked good enough to eat.

"Where is my son?" He stood tall and strong in her living room. The man wasn't there for anything other than his child.

That was clear.

"You don't seem like you're having a good day."

"My son. Where is he?" He looked over her head into the house.

His words were hard and quick.

"He's in the bedroom. Do you want me to go get him?"

"That's what the fuck I'm here for right?"

He had been in there less than a minute and already she felt like a failure.

When she dropped a napkin, she was holding, by accident on the way to Baltimore's room, she looked behind herself and caught him staring.

He took in each curve of her body.

Her heart tripped a beat because dropping the napkin was an accident, but it had given her such a gift.

She caught the nigga slippin'.

There was something about her that he still longed for, and it was all in his eyes.

And that gave her hope.

The way she felt, that was all she needed.

Twenty minutes passed and he was playing with his son in the living room when she said, "Are you hungry?"

"I'm eating later."

"I made some Spanish rice and chicken. How you like it."

He looked up at her once. "I said I'll have my chef cook me something later."

"Ok."

He looked over at her briefly and back at Baltimore. "And why you wearing that tonight?"

"Because I knew you wouldn't stay long, and I wanted to be ready for bed."

That was a lie.

Ace told her what to say and she was glad he did.

"I don't want no niggas around my son."

That was the first time he ever said that to her.

And so she believed she was making more strides.

"I will never have a nigga around your son. I will never have a nigga around me either."

135

She wasn't certain but she could see what appeared to be a half smile move upward in the corner of his mouth. On the opposite side from where she was sitting.

Fifteen minutes passed and they were having a good time.

In her mind anyway, until her roommate slid from the back like a snake.

What happened to the pills she was supposed to have popped which would put her out for a long time?

"Oh ain't that sweet." Sydney slurred. "Look at the father with his son."

"Go in your room Sydney you're drunk." Aliyah said standing up from the sofa.

Instead of going into her room she moved closer to the trio. "I just want to say hi to your ex-boyfriend."

Walid looked at Aliyah and then Sydney. "Everything okay with y'all? 'Cause you look out of it, Sydney."

"She fine." Aliyah said.

"I was asking her."

"She just drunk that's all."

"Where is Roman?"

"I don't know."

He stood up. "What you mean?"

"He's with his friend. For a playdate."

"There is a lot of play dating going on around here." Aliyah snatched her towards the hallway and into her bedroom. Closing the door, she knocked her to the bed.

With both hands on her neck, nails digging into her flesh she said, "If you destroy this for me and get my son taken away, I will kill you. Do you hear me? With my bare hands, I will kill you!"

CHAPTER SEVENTEEN
NO LOVE

Ever since Banks was married the breakfast routine vanished.

Back in the day nothing was more important than bringing everyone together and sitting at a table over a meal catered by world renowned chefs.

But lately Banks seemed too busy with dollars, websites, and cryptocurrency to spend time with his family.

Everyone noticed too.

At one point family seemed to be everything to him. He literally built the island for them to escape from madness in America.

But now, the family appeared to be a nuisance to Banks.

And so Mason and Joey sat, drinking coffee, while speaking of the only thing that plagued Mason's mind as the ocean sang in the background.

Alone.

"You used to be so much fun." Joey said. "Let's hit the streets again. I found this new club in Belize that–."

"What are you five years old?"

Joey's heart hurt. He loved rolling with Mason's smooth ass. "I'm telling you, Uncle Mason the nigga is still in Mexico. I know you don't want to hear it but it's true."

"I...I know I can overreact. But I saw the hate in that boy's eyes. And if I know anything about hate, it's that if it's strong enough, it can act as a motivator."

"We good."

Mason nodded. "I hear you."

"But there's something else going on, I wanted to run past you." Joey said.

He poured himself another cup of coffee. "What's up?"

"I heard Patrick tell Bolt something very wild."

"They always talking about something, but I'm listening."

"Before I say anything, I want you to know that I was going to go to Spacey, but this family got too much going on as is. And Spacey goes from zero to a hundred over Riot. So we gotta spread this shit out. At the same time somebody else needs to know but me."

"You're driving me crazy. Now, what is it?"

"When I walked past Patrick's room, I heard him say something about taking out Riot. Because if he did, then maybe he would get an inheritance. What was he talking about?"

Mason knew exactly what he was referring to.

Banks made it clear that only his bloodline would get part of the money in the event something happened to him. Which meant his own heirs were left with almost nothing.

Ordinarily he wouldn't care but Banks and his bond was built on teenage beef. Which ultimately grew into two grown men hating one another. But he didn't want the same for the younger generation.

"The other day Banks for whatever reason said that if something were to happen to him, he would leave all the money to only the Wales'. Which means the Louisville's get nothing."

Joey laughed.

"I'm not catching the humor."

"You know pops would take care of y'all. I don't know what got into him but if he said it, he playing."

"You know I'm not concerned about money. I've been off that a long time ago. And if it wasn't for the boys it wouldn't even be a thought. But whether he's playing or not I got children."

"I don't want to be weird here because to be honest I like to stay out of this situation. But I know for a fact that pops would not let things go without taking care of you and the boys."

"What does that mean?"

"So we're going to act like at one point my father wasn't your wife? We really going to do that?"

Mason moved uneasily in his seat. "Joey, you weren't there. In the gym. He basically said that you guys would be fine, but my people won't. Now I have no illusions that I won't live well for the rest of my life with my current funds. But I need my seeds to be financially secure when it's my time to go."

"I feel you."

"This ain't about greed."

"I know it's not. Do you want me to talk to him?"

"What are y'all rapping about?" Banks said entering with Faye.

"Nothing." Mason said, sipping his coffee.

"The thing is I'm not talking to you." He pointed his way. "Remember you said you had no words for me. So let's just leave it at that."

"You know–."

"I'll tell him." Joey said, trying to break it up. "It's not that deep."

"I'm listening." Banks responded.

"It's about Ace. I verified that he was still there. In Mexico."

Mason didn't know what he expected him to say but he certainly didn't expect him to lie. The shit held a lot of problems for the family so he couldn't let that ride.

"You didn't verify anything, Joey." Mason said.

"No but I got enough info to tell me pop's is right." He said to Mason. "That's all we were talking about."

Mason wasn't going to leave things as is.

If Joey wanted to protect him he could. But at least something was going to come out of him talking to him for the moment.

"That's actually not what we were talking about. Do you not realize because of you making my family feel like they aren't a part of this family as a whole that you turned them against one another?"

"Make it clear, Mason."

"Is my bloodline a part of this family or not?"

"Maybe I should go to our bedroom." Faye said.

"Yeah, do that!" Mason directed her.

"Do not yell at my young wife!"

"If she was old it would be good?" Mason laughed.

"Nigga, what?"

"Let me find out you gotta justify being married."

"Mason, you pushing it."

142

"Then answer the question! Is my family a part of this family or not!"

"Let's talk out in the hallway."

"Let's go then!" Mason responded, jumping up.

When they stormed out Joey sat at the table and Faye slowly approached and joined him. They could be heard yelling from the hallway.

"I hope whatever is going on won't break them up. I don't know all the details about their bond, but I hear they've been friends for such a long time."

Suddenly Joey started laughing. He could tell she was fishing.

"What is it?" She said.

"You're relatively new to this family but know this. Hell would freeze over twice before they stopped being friends. Granted we haven't had this sort of beef in our family in a long time. But I still feel strongly that we may all go away but the two of them will always be."

His statement made her very uncomfortable. "What does that mean? Why are they so close?"

He stood up. "Ask your husband. I've said enough." He walked out.

CHAPTER EIGHTEEN
POP THAT SHIT

Aliyah was fast asleep when suddenly she felt a warm body behind her. A light smile spread on her face, and she pushed her ass back into the warm presence and moaned.

"That's nice," she said. "You don't know how good it feels to have you back in my bed." Her body grew tingly everywhere as she continued to feel his warm heat on her back. "I miss this so much."

"Is that right?"

Jumping up quickly she turned on the night lamp and looked at who was seated on her mattress.

It was Ace.

He was wearing a white t-shirt, blue jeans, and light tinted shades. The man looked fine but who gave a fuck? "Hey, baby girl."

"What are you doing in my fucking house?" She grabbed the sheets and covered her body. "And how did you get inside?"

"I came to see you."

She snatched more blankets, while standing in the corner. "I didn't give you the authorization to get in my bed, Ace. I don't know what's going on, but you can't do this. How did you get in anyway?"

"You need to lower your voice. I don't want that pussy." He said firmly. "But I will kill you if I must. I already feel like your friend in the back will be a problem. Don't make me get rid of her first by putting her out of her misery."

"My friend? She's your baby mother too."

He laughed. "Fuck that slut."

She took a deep breath. "What do you want?"

"I came to tell you that you did a good job tonight. My brother may not have said it, but I could see in his eyes that he was excited about the possibility of y'all getting back together. So keep applying pressure."

"You could see me? Do you have my house bugged?" She dropped the sheet, jumped into some black stretch pants and a red top as she ran around her room, touching any and everything to find the camera.

He laughed.

"What the fuck is funny, Ace?"

"I had this house bugged before you even lived here. Originally I did it to find out what was going on with Joey and Sydney. Before I was sent to Mexico. But he proved to be the most boring out of my brothers so nothing came of it. Especially when he left her ass. After

145

that I just looked at the recordings whenever I wanted to make sure both of you were here. So I heard about the party you all were having and decided to pop up. Due to the cameras, I knew the perfect time to snatch them little niggas and everything."

She was trembling with rage. "You will pay for this. I don't know how but you will."

He waved the air. "I came by to tell you it's time for you to go a little bit harder. Several times my brother looked at you with lust when you didn't know it. But you were always too focused on something else."

"That's because you came into our lives and took our sons."

"Call it what you want. But I need you to make him fall. Harder. And that means getting him in your bed. And fucking him. Do I make myself clear?"

Silence.

"Remember that your son is in my care. And I'm a temperamental sort of nigga. Don't fuck with me."

Patrick was sitting in his room with Melanie. She was Riot's girlfriend.

He told her earlier in the day that Riot wanted to talk to her about something serious. And so he and Bolt sent a car to pick her up. Now that she was there sitting on his bed she was getting antsy.

Besides, what was going on?

After rolling up some weed and passing it back and forth with her he blew smoke in the air and said, "Is it true that you never slept with my cousin?"

"He told you that?"

"Yeah. So I think he's going to break up with you." He put the weed in the ashtray and went to his balcony and allowed some ocean breeze to seep in. Her long brown hair blew lightly.

"He's going to break up with me? Just because I won't fuck him. Because he didn't seem to have a problem with it before."

"Well rich niggas change."

"But...but we're both young so I told him that we would probably do something like that once we went to the prom. He seemed to be cool to me."

"So you calling me a liar?"

"No, but–"

"Look, other girls aren't waiting to give up the pussy. Other girls are more mature. So this game you playing ain't doing you no favors. Know what I mean?"

Patrick unfortunately was just like his deceased father.

He had deep-seated desires to manipulate people to get what he wanted. And if he didn't get what he wanted he would create a situation where so much confusion would arise that would end with him being the victor.

Suddenly she started crying softly. "I texted him several times and he didn't answer any of my messages."

Patrick knew why he didn't answer it.

He had taken his phone earlier that day to prevent her from reaching out. And now Bolt had it under his bed and was waiting for part two of his plan.

"I don't want to break up with him. What can I do?"

"I'm going to go and get him later. First you need training."

"I don't understand."

"He said he's done so that means it's over. But if you do what I tell you, then he will change his mind."

She looked down. "I'm so confused."

"You ever went down on somebody before? Because you gotta learn that first since you fucking with a Wales nigga."

"Do you mean to put that thing in my mouth?"

Patrick gripped himself. "Yeah. You got a pretty mouth. It would be a shame if you don't know how to use it."

"No. It sounds nasty."

He glared. "If you do that for him I'm sure he'll stay with you. But you still sound immature, so I don't know if it's a waste of time anyway. Maybe Riot was right for leaving you alone."

"I didn't say I didn't want to. I said I don't know how. This all sounds so crazy because it's different from what we talked about."

"That's because you're not a dude. He talks like this to dudes. So I'm giving you an insight on how his mind works." He knocked on his temples with his fist.

"I guess."

"You want me to teach you?"

"By putting your thing in my mouth?"

"Can you stop making it sound like it's a snake or something? You sure you don't like to deal with girls instead? 'Cause you sounding gay."

"No!"

"So let me teach you just long enough for him to make sure you can handle it all."

"This feels wrong. I'm pretty sure you're lying. Because the Riot I know would never do this to me. I don't know why you're being so mean but I'm out of here!"

Patrick hadn't expected her to be so smart.

In fact, there was a running joke that she will believe anything you told her. They've seen it happen on more than one occasion. But he made a mistake in believing she would be stupid enough to fall for *his* trap.

She got up to move towards the door. "I'm out of here."

"Are you sure about that? Because if you go then I'll tell my cousin we had sex anyway. Then he definitely won't deal with you anymore."

She turned around and faced him. "He won't believe you!"

"You're in my room. And he don't know." She shrugged. "Why wouldn't he believe me?"

Her eyes widened and tears rolled down her face. "Why you doing this?"

"Like I said, I'm trying to teach you. If you stop thinking the worst in me then you could understand that. But go on and leave. We'll see what happens to your relationship with Riot in the future after I tell him you couldn't keep your hands off me."

This scared her. "Okay. What do I have to do?"

He unfastened his pants and stomped his foot for Bolt to start the recording.

When they were done getting the footage of her sucking his dick, they left the video on Riot's phone. And then put it back into his room.

———✈———

Blakeslee held the phone to her ear and she looked out her window which overlooked the beach. Her friend, back in the States, was telling her the most amazing news she heard in a long time.

Ace was back!

When she first told her friend that she would know who she was looking for in front of Sydney's house, her friend assumed she was talking about Walid. She called several times to say that Walid had popped up.

Each time she hit her, Blakeslee would say no, that's not what she's waiting on.

And then Blakeslee got the call she was anticipating.

"It's him! It's fucking him!"

Blakeslee said, "Walid?"

"No! Ace! It's Ace's fine ass!"

"Listen, you have to get in touch with him. You have to give him my number."

"I don't know if you want to do that. He looks different. Meaner. Blond streaks in his hair. A walk that doesn't seem natural. I mean, don't get me wrong, I still wanna fuck him but–."

"Just do what I'm asking!" She yelled. "And different or not he's still my brother! And he would want to hear from me!"

"I got to be honest." She breathed deeply. "I'm scared."

"Girl, cut the shit."

"What are you talking about!"

"Bitch, how much do you want? Because we both know why you holding out. Y'all always hitting up Wales niggas for a payday."

"That's not fair, Blakeslee."

"I'm serious! How much do you want?"

She was silent for a moment and then she whispered, "$5000."

"Speak up!"

"I said $5,000 would be great."

"You got it! Money ain't a big thing. *If* you give me his number or give him mine, you'll get paid!"

"Done!"

CHAPTER NINETEEN
SIBLING RIVALRY

A ce sat in his car, in front of Aliyah and Sydney's house. Crickets and the sound of vehicles driving in the distance kept him busy.

It was well after midnight, and he was looking for signs of his brother. But he had yet to come see his son and he was getting tired. He could have stayed longer but the last thing he wanted was to hear Arbella's whining.

If he wasn't in the bed when she rolled over, she would cause problems in the brothel.

Knocking on doors.

Throwing whores off their Johns looking for his face.

All the while believing he was cheating.

So time was of the essence.

He was just about to pull off when from the passenger's side window someone said, "Excuse me. Are you Blakeslee's brother?"

Ace was caught slipping. "Who the fuck are you?"

"You don't know me but I'm a friend of your sister."

He quickly jumped out the car and snatched her. Stuffing her inside of his vehicle he aimed the gun in her direction. "Stay right there!"

"O...okay."

He rushed to his side of the car. Still aiming he said, "You really shouldn't have done that. I got a lot of shit going on and the last thing I needed was seeing a stranger asking about me."

She was trembling. "But...didn't you hear me? I'm a friend of your sisters. I would not have bothered you but she begged me to. Even paid me for it. Please don't hurt me though."

"It doesn't matter who you are. You should not have approached me."

She started crying on sight.

Loud too.

Afraid someone would see and hear them he said, "Shut the fuck up!" He brought down the handle on the side of her forehead.

Blood splashed everywhere but the girl acted as if she didn't know it.

Adrenaline was too high.

"I'm trying." She wiped blood away from approaching her eye. "But I told your sister I didn't want to do this. She begged me though. Said she really needed to get in contact with you."

The last time he saw Blakeslee they didn't end on good terms. Primarily because she was sleeping around and bringing strange men into his home. While underaged. Something he told her he would not tolerate if she lived with him.

"I don't have anything to say to Blakeslee right now."

"Okay you want me to tell her that?" She wiped more blood away. Now the shit was starting to hurt.

He was about to kill her and be done with it until he thought about the situation. Maybe the girl could be of some use to him in the future. "Call my sister. Right now."

"But it's early in-."

"Now!"

She quickly removed the phone from her pocket and made the phone call. Every so often she would look over at him. She wasn't certain but something said he was mad enough to snap her neck at any time.

"Blakeslee, I'm here with your brother," she said with a quivering voice.

"Are you serious?" She whispered. "Put him on. Quickly!"

"She wants to talk to you." She said, extending the bloody phone in his direction.

He took it from her, wiped the blood away and said, "How you been?"

Suddenly she started crying. He didn't know what he expected her to do but crying was not it.

She wept for their relationship being over.

"Blakeslee, I'm going to need you to stop. I don't mind speaking to you but you have to talk to me clearly so I can understand what it is you want from me."

"I'm sorry I'm not trying to cry but–"

"You are crying though. And that's the last thing I need right now."

She sniffled. "You're right. I'm just so happy to hear from you that's all."

"Why did you want to get in contact with me?"

"Are you serious?"

"I'm waiting on an answer."

"I wanted to get in touch with you because I haven't spoken to you in like forever. I wanted to get in touch with you because I miss you! Is it such a bad thing?"

"You know I'm on fucked up terms with your father. And you also know he likes people to pick a side. When you moved out without telling me, you chose him over me."

156

"So you're acting like he's not your father?"

He glared. "You heard me."

"So what you doing there? In the States. Do you have a plan?"

"I'm growing annoyed! What is it?"

"I told you I missed you."

"It's something more."

"I swear it isn't."

"Blakeslee, I'm going to say something to you. And I need you just to listen."

"Okay. Anything you say."

"Have you told anyone that I'm here?"

"What you mean?"

"Blakeslee."

"No. Of course not."

"Are you lying to me?"

"Ace, I–"

"Cabello."

"Cabello who?"

He shifted a little in his seat. And he definitely didn't feel like losing time on what was happening with Walid and Aliyah. "That's the name I go by now. Cabello."

"Oh. I like it."

He didn't give a fuck.

He dragged one hand down his face. "Keep my whereabouts a secret. Or when everything comes together, I'll come for you too."

"Of course, Ace. I mean, Cabello."

"How will I know when you need me?"

"I'll come find you."

Ace walked into the brothel.

As he walked up the stairs he could hear women and men moaning from behind the closed doors. He'd heard these things before but he got aroused this time.

Maybe it was everything that was happening.

Maybe it was the fact that he was finally getting closer to what he wanted.

Revenge.

Whatever it was he sought after his fuck partner and a few seconds later he happened upon her door.

The window was open as the moonlight shone through; Arbella was asleep on her side. From her head to her waist, it dipped ever so lightly. She looked like an hourglass lying on its side.

He wanted her.

Badly.

To get to the pussy, he removed his clothing and snuck up behind her.

When she felt his presence, she backed into him. Ass first of course.

Taking his dick out of his boxers he stroked it a few times before it stiffened in his palm. Wasting no time, he eased into her from behind like a ball on a bowling alley.

"I miss you so much." She moaned.

He didn't feel like talking. Instead, he continued to stroke softly back and forth.

Back and forth.

If there was nothing else that could be said, their love language was consistent. And both were fluent.

With each push and pull she got greasier. Wetter. Warmer. He lifted her ass cheek high so he could look at the pussy from another angle.

It was pretty.

Pink.

Wet.

"Nigga, I been waiting on this dick all night," she said.

"Is that right?"

He reached in front of her and grabbed her throat. Squeezing while he pumped, he was almost there. "I'm about to…I'm about to…"

"Me too," he announced, feeling a flood coming on.

When he was ready, he removed his dick from her warmth and bust all over the side of her hip.

Cream dripped down like glaze icing on a cake. "You could have stayed inside."

"Nah. I want our baby to be born in royalty. In money. Like I was. Not in a whorehouse."

"I get it."

"It'll all happen soon though."

"I swear to God I can't wait."

CHAPTER TWENTY
A SECRET

Walid was at Sydney's house, looking at Baltimore play in the backyard when Sydney came outside.

"Oh...you're still here." She was drunk and appeared off step.

"Are you okay?" He kept his eyes on her. Because something about her was off and he was trying to figure out what. While also wanting to steer clear of her personal bullshit.

"Why you asking me if I'm okay? Like you care. I don't know what it is with you Wales boys. But I can tell you believe you think you own the world. And that the rest of us are pawns."

"We do own the world. So what's your point?"

"So you don't deny it?"

"It's not about denying it. It's facts. But you're drunk so you can't see that right now. And I don't waste my time speaking to drunks. So if you want to tell me something, open your mouth and talk. Or get the fuck out my face. Because I'm already growing bored with you."

She took a deep breath and looked down before looking back up at him. "Can I trust you?"

"You have to answer that question yourself."

"I need to know if I can trust you before we go any further. I know it may seem that I'm under the influence and I am. But I have some information that you may–"

"Sydney, what's going on?" Walid snapped. "Does this have anything to do with my son? Is she bringing niggas around my boy?"

She planned to talk about her own son, but it was obvious that once again the only thing he cared about was his. "That's all that concerns you? Baltimore. What about Roman?"

"The family already decided on that situation. So I don't get involved."

"So they really have written him off?"

In that moment it was clear that she had nothing or no one. And so the pain she was feeling inside ripped at her in all kinds of ways.

"What did you think would happen? You came in between brothers. I know you felt like Joey wasn't going to be about you but if you had given him a little time you would've realized we stay loyal. But the moment you do us wrong you dead to us. Now, that's what the

162

family feels. But can you tell me right now is nephew okay? Should I know–"

"What you doing out here, Sydney?" Aliyah said walking out onto the patio.

Sydney looked at her with wide eyes and ran into the house.

"What is up with that bitch?"

"Why she have to be all that?"

"I don't trust her. And I'm tired of the games that's being played around here. Now what is going on? Is she on drugs?"

He was getting antsy and she had to think quickly if she was going to stick to the plan to make him fall in love again. "I miss you."

He took a step to the right and left. She caught him off guard. "What you talking about?"

"I miss you, Walid. I made a mistake when I said I didn't want you anymore. And every day leading up to that point has been torture."

"What does this have to do with what's happening with Sydney?"

"Because she thinks that if you want me too, that you would take us away. Back to Belize. And if you took us away she would no longer be able to have access to the funds."

"My father would never take Roman off the account. That's in Mason's honor. Even if he doesn't acknowledge or claim him."

"I told her the same thing, but she doesn't believe me. I even told her you don't want me anymore. So I don't know why she's so upset. It's not like you're going to have a second heart. Right? I'm crazy for thinking like this aren't I?"

He moved uneasily.

"Do you want me again, Walid? At this point I'll take anything you say but I just want to hear your words. Whatever they are. It took me a lot to even try and talk to you."

"I'm here about my son."

"Answer the question."

"I don't owe you an answer, bitch! You stood in my face and told me you didn't want to be with me anymore. And I told you I was done with you then. Why would I walk that back?"

"But are you done with me now?"

"I mean, why you playing these games, Aliyah? You think I'm a weak ass nigga or something?"

"There has never been anybody else to make me feel the way you do."

"So you've been bringing dudes around my son?"

She stepped closer. "Never have I ever brought another man around your child. Ever! I'm a good mother. Say what you want but you can attest to that."

"But you have been seeing other men, right?"

She felt it was a trap.

A way for him to deny what he felt if he felt anything at all. Admitting it would be blown up into her looking like a whore. At the same time there was no need for her lying. If she wanted to gain his trust she had to start with the truth.

"Yeah, I've been seeing people but nothing like what we had."

Walid walked away and leaned against the side of the house.

"What's wrong?" She asked.

Was he into his feelings? She thought.

Was Ace right?

Based on the look on his face she was starting to think he couldn't express himself in a true way.

"When I left you promised that you could do what needed to be done to see about my boy. Here in the States. And I trusted you the entire time."

Oh, no!

Things were backfiring!

165

"And it's true! I can take care of our child!" She trembled.

"Nah. Because now I'm starting to believe that the only reason you wanted to keep my son here was so I could possibly come back to you."

"Walid, I promise you that isn't it. I love being a mother."

"Then what the fuck is all this you talking about now?"

She walked over to him and dropped to her knees. "Please, hear my voice."

"Get off of me."

"Please don't leave me." She tugged at his waist and he could feel himself stiffening.

"Please, give me another chance."

"Fuck is wrong with you." She looked and smelled so good he was getting sick.

"I miss you. I made a mistake. What do I have to do to get you back? That's the only thing that this is about right now."

Slowly she rose and wrapped her arms around his body.

It was the first time she held him since they broke up. When she placed her head and ear against his chest, she could hear his heart thumping.

166

Pounding.

He still wants me. She thought.

"I got a new girl. I just threw her a party for her birthday and everything. Going to link back up with her after I see about my son today."

She peeled herself off his body. "What did you just say?"

"I said I got a new girl. And you and I are done." He walked toward the door. "I'll see about my son later to tuck him into bed." He rolled out.

She dropped to her knees crying.

The Shaman and Blakeslee were in her room doing her makeup.

She was so excited that her brother was back even though she didn't know why. The way the family was treating her she didn't care what he had planned. Just as long as he included her in some way.

Sharon was finishing up her makeup and said, "Okay tell me again what you about to do."

She pouted her lips. "What you told me to do. Seduce."

"But I already put a spell on him."

"So things should be easier if I add a little more of my appeal."

"Girl, your appeal is trash. You didn't even know the man wanted you before I told you so."

"It doesn't matter because I know now." She winked at her.

"I don't mean to keep bringing it up but..."

"Please don't say it."

"What about the dog?"

"I'm not going to tell you again about that dog. If I get what I want, understand that you'll get what you want too. But not before that."

"Okay I guess I have to wait."

"I guess you do." Blakeslee stood up and ran her hands down her curvy hips. Smiling at herself in the mirror she walked out.

She thought it would be hard to find Mason, but he was sitting on the deck behind their house smoking weed and drinking a glass of whiskey.

She looked down at her body once more to be sure it was appealing to the opposite sex. There was not an ounce of cellulite on her skin.

She was fit.

Toned.

And beautiful.

Of course he's going to be attracted to me. She thought.

"Mason." Blakeslee said, sliding outside.

The moment he saw her he looked away with guilt. "What is it? I was kind of hoping I could spend a few moments alone."

"I'm sorry to bother you, but I need you to help me."

His gaze fell on her. "For someone who says they need help, you sure look fine to me."

"Thank you. I think."

He took a deep breath. "Like I said, to be honest I'm not in the mood for company. I hope you understand."

"I believe I know why you're sad."

He glared. "What you talking about?"

"Everybody's rapping about how you and my father aren't speaking. I know how it feels to be alone. And I know it may be annoying how I rely on you for support. But literally you're all I have. We have each other."

"It's not about being sad. I just have to make some decisions that I didn't think I would at this point in my life."

"Do you want to share, Mason? With me?"

Silence.

"I understand."

He looked at her again and then looked downward. "You know what, what I'm going through has nothing to do with you. And I'm sorry I'm taking it out on you. So come closer. Tell me what you want."

She glided in his direction and stood in front of him. "I need you to help me be more likable."

He laughed and looked away. "You're coming to me with this?"

"Yeah. What's funny?"

"Before you and Ace, I was the family villain. So I'm the last person that can tell you how to be *likable*."

"Actually, that makes you the best person. I don't really know about all the stories in the past when everyone was living in the States. Nobody likes talking to me. But I do know that at one point you weren't considered trustworthy. And now everybody loves you. I want that for myself." She sat next to him.

"Blakeslee, I-."

"Please. Help me."

"Why don't you ask Minnesota?"

"Because Minnesota is busy with my daughter and that dumb ass dog."

His eyes fell on her again. He was trying to determine if what he detected was guilt or something else.

"She'll be fine. I'm talking about Sugar."

She nodded. "She'll also hate me for the rest of her life. I'm sure."

"Big families like the one we have, especially those that are blended like ours breed this level of hate."

"But why?"

"I don't have all the answers, but I believe it has something to do with this... when you have different personalities, and you see how others move in the world versus how you move yourself it's easy to develop a complex. You watch people interact with other people in the family and wonder why you don't get the same reception. It's life."

"I think I understand."

"So...what kind of help do you want from me?"

"For starters tell me what I'm doing wrong."

He looked around and back at her. "Well, sometimes you don't know what to say out your mouth. To be honest I'm not sure this can be taught. But, that's the first step. Filter yourself. You gotta work on that. But there is hope. It was that way with me too and it took me a long time to change."

She didn't get it. "What do I say wrong around here?"

"It's not what you say, it's when you say it. Just because a thought moves you it doesn't mean everybody has to know. Resist the urge to tell people what's in your heart all the time."

"I thought that was a good thing. To tell people what's on your heart."

"It's good for people who aren't always giving it that way. But for those of you who are always saying something all the time you can make people angry. And uncomfortable when they are around you."

"Are you uncomfortable around me?"

"Nah, shawty. I'm good."

She placed a hand on his lap.

His dick jumped.

"That's good because you are all I have in this house. And I'm going to try to do what you tell me. But if it doesn't work, you are enough for me."

Banks was on his way out on the deck but stopped short at the sliding glass door when he saw his daughter holding Mason's hand.

His heart dropped.

And he wondered what was going on between them.

Mason was in the lounge drinking whiskey in the soft leather recliner when Banks walked inside.

"Can I join you?" Banks asked.

"Uh...actually I..." he relaxed into the seat. "On second thought, come on in."

Banks poured himself a glass of whiskey and sat in the other recliner belonging to him. "I'm going to say something to you that's going to be hard to voice." He took a large sip. "But you need to hear it."

"Okay."

"You need to stop all this being jealous of me bullshit."

He frowned. "Being jealous of you?"

"You heard me, nigga!" He yelled. "I see you around here consoling my children, trying to play hero. No matter what you do, you will never be me." He pointed at himself.

Mason was devastated. "Brother, I wished for you greatness all my life. You got this-."

"I built this land. I made this money! Me! And if you can't deal with that, and how I handle the situations even with Ace, then that's your problem not mine."

Silence.

"Well, what do you have to say?"

Mason drank what was left in his glass. "Nothing, brother. You said it all."

CHAPTER TWENTY-ONE
FLIGHT PLAN

Mason was supposed to be taking Blakeslee out later that night to help her with her people skills.

But before he left the house he knew he had to speak to his son and grandson about a few things that would change their lives.

When he arrived at Patrick's door he knocked once and turned the knob. "Grandpop's! Why you ain't tell me you were coming inside?"

"I did." He walked deeper inside. "I got to talk to you about something."

Patrick rose from the bed. "Uh.... what's going on?" He shifted from left to right and Mason could tell he was guilty. "I'm listening."

"We moving."

"Wait...why?"

"I have some plans for a future for all of us back home. And I want to take advantage of these deals."

"But...but I don't wanna leave." Patrick said.

"Me either," Bolt chimed in.

"You have no choice." He paused. "Get your things together. Take what you really need. We can replace everything else."

"Grandpops, please! I don't–"

"It's settled."

He was about to leave when he doubled back. "Before I forget, what's going on with you and Riot?"

Patrick shuffled a little, still upset about the turn of events. "It's not my fault! For real! His girl been wanting me. And things got out of control."

Mason frowned because this was new. "What you talking about?"

"His girlfriend. She wanted to get with me, and I tried to let him know but he ain't believe me. So now we beefing."

Upon hearing this news Mason felt that what Joey told him about Patrick wanting to take Riot's life was all around a female. If that was the case he was sure he could talk him down. After all, his future plans to move would prevent him from acting on any indiscretions anyway.

"I don't know what's going on with y'all but you have to remember you're family. Fuck the dumb shit."

"So you're not mad?"

How could he be?

He didn't know about the oral sex trap video. He legit thought it was light beefing shit.

"I'm not mad. Why would I be? Cousins and brothers go through this kind of thing. The key is how you act on it that matters." He pointed at him. "You may be wanting to do a lot of things while moving off emotions. Just remember what you mean to Riot."

Silence.

For some reason Mason thought about Banks and their heated conversation yesterday. And so his own words played on repeat in his mind.

Remember who you are to him. He thought.

"Grandpops, you okay?"

"Oh, yeah. Like I was saying. He's family despite the absence of a bloodline. Don't let anything get in the way of that."

When he turned around he was surprised to see Riot there. His chest was rising and falling heavily as he looked around Mason at Patrick.

Mason considered stepping in but figured after having the conversation with his grandson that things would work out okay.

So he tapped him on the shoulder and walked off.

But shit wasn't okay.

Riot stormed deeper into the room and slammed the door. "I saw the video in my phone! I saw what you did to my girlfriend."

Patrick grinned.

"So you think this is funny?" Riot continued.

"I think it's hilarious actually." He rubbed his hands together. "You claim to own everything around here but I guess you don't own your bitch's mouth. After all, well, you saw the video." He grabbed his dick. "She sucked it good too."

"You gonna pay for doing that shit."

"Am I?"

"I promise you will pay." He ran off.

Blakeslee was on the phone in Mason's Aston Martin talking to Patrick, with Bolt in the background complaining.

"Slow down," she said. "I don't understand what y'all trying to say."

"Grandpops said we moving."

Her eyes widened. "Moving where? And why?"

"I don't know but I don't wanna live in the States. I want to stay here! On Wales Island."

Blakeslee felt weak.

Mason was truly the only person in her mind who cared about her. So the fact that he was leaving hurt deeply.

"Give me some time, I'll come up with a plan to change his mind."

"How can you be sure?"

"Just trust me. That's all I can say for now."

Spacey was walking in the corridor leading to the exit when he saw Mason about to leave the mansion for his outing with Blakeslee.

"Unc, let me holla at you."

"What's up?" Blakeslee was in his car waiting on him.

"I wanna rap to you about you and pops."

Mason took a deep breath. "You need to leave that thing alone. Besides, I got some place to be."

"I'ma be straight up." He said. "You scaring me."

"Why would I scare you?"

Spacey breathed heavily. "When I was younger, I couldn't stand you. To be honest it's weird having to state the obvious. But it's true. And then we went from weird to a close bond I still respect to this day. I mean you literally took up for me against your own son." He moved closer to prevent anyone else from hearing his words. "I don't speak about that often. When he raped me. But it stays on my mind."

"I'm following."

"I heard the fight you were having with my father in the lounge. And I don't like the distance between you two. I really hope y'all make it right before things get too late."

"Whatever goes on between me and Banks I don't want you worrying about. It won't change how I feel about you."

He laughed. "Not the classic divorce talk."

Mason laughed.

It did sound as if he was preparing to break up with Banks.

"I'm serious. But your father is making moves for him and his future. And I have to make some moves for me and mine. Starting with getting the boys to America and making sure Roman is good. Which is why I want you to take me back to the States in a couple of days.

Already made arrangements with River in Bmore, so we can leave without any issues when it's time."

Spacey stepped back and covered his mouth with his hand. "Are you saying you're separating the Louisville and the Wales Clan? After all these years."

"Will you take me to the States or not?"

"You know I will but–"

"I'll talk to you later. Don't worry. Things will work out." He walked out the door.

Leaving Spacey stuck.

CHAPTER TWENTY-TWO
BABY MAMA WET

The crickets sang in the background...

Walid had placed Baltimore in his bed for the night.

Taking a second, he stood in the doorway and looked at what he and Aliyah made. The boy was perfect in his eyes, and he couldn't wait to shower all his love onto him fully.

Aliyah walked up behind him. "He looks just like you."

He jumped a little.

"I didn't know you to be anxious." She spoke.

Normally he wasn't.

But he could feel that she wanted something from him he wasn't prepared to give. "I'm about to leave. I'm going to stay for a few days and then I'm headed back to the island. We have to talk before I do."

"Okay, Walid."

He nodded.

"And, Walid..." she whispered, moving a bit closer.

"If you need anything let me know I can put more money in the account. So you can–"

"Walid, don't go yet, baby." She moved behind him and placed her arms around his waist. Squeezing with all her heart she said, "Please don't leave. Please give me another chance. I know you said you have a girl, but she can't mean to you what I do. Because we have history. Love. A son."

He tried to walk around her. "I gotta get out of here."

Closer.

"Walid...don't make me beg. Her pussy not wetter than mine. It can't be."

The moment he turned around she increased her height by standing on her tiptoes.

Kissing him softly she could feel him melt like ice in front of a hot blow dryer under her touch.

"What you doing, girl?"

"Applying pressure."

"Don't play with me."

"Come get this pussy, boy. Please."

His minty tongue slid inside of her mouth as he gripped the sides of her face.

"You know you still want this...tell me I'm lying."

Their kiss tasted like fresh water from a stream.

Cool at first and then warm.

"Don't leave me." She whispered while their mouths were still connected. "I'll sleep with your dick inside my pussy. Inside of my mouth."

When she positioned her body as if she was about to jump up, he caught her. Her legs dangled along the sides of his hips.

Wanting to feel her, with one hand holding her up, he closed the bedroom door and walked down the corridor.

Neither one of them could see Sydney sitting on her bed with the door open. But she saw them walk by as they made it to Aliyah's room.

And she hated them both for it.

With one knee on the bed followed by the other one, he gently laid her on her back while his body remained on top of hers.

This kiss was long.

Passionate.

Their bodies pressed together produced heat high enough to cook a meal. He was stiffened a long time ago. The moment she begged for his love. Which was one of the reasons why he wanted to leave her house. But she wouldn't let him.

Just kept applying pressure like Ace said.

Kept asking for the dick.

Aliyah was right about one thing.

He definitely still had feelings for her although he couldn't express what those feelings were.

Without wasting any more time, he removed his dick and pressed into her body. It wasn't like she belonged to him officially. For all he knew many men could have enjoyed her flesh.

But he knew who her owner really was.

And so, deeper, and deeper he moved into her body.

She was so wet now that the bed was soaked underneath both of them. His pants weren't even all the way off but he positioned one foot on the mattress followed by the other.

At first her legs lay open like a wishbone. But now one leg dangled over his shoulder so he could hit the pussy right.

As they made love, slowly, they looked into each other's eyes.

It was a look filled with longing and regrets of things said in the past.

Personally, Aliyah didn't know what was to happen between them. But she did know that she would cherish this moment as if he had taken her back. Sure he took care of her financially.

But Aliyah wanted his love.

She wanted his last name.

Whether Ace forced her to or not she hoped things would end for the better. Besides, she dreamed of this moment. She heard somewhere that even the wicked could bring a manifestation into picture. Maybe Walid's wicked twin did for her what she always desired.

Bring him back to her bed.

Back to her life.

"I belong to you!" She exclaimed as her body started to tingle.

"I know you do."

"I'm so sorry, Walid," she said as her body trembled so hard her head began to ache. "I made a mistake letting you go."

He turned her over, so he could see her pretty ass hiked up in the air. Mountain high. It was nice and bubbly.

She had certainly taken care of herself; he could give her that. If he could give her nothing else.

"I'm...I'm cumming," she announced.

That was quick but it made sense.

"Hold that shit, baby. Wait on me."

"I...I can't...I..."

He knew she exploded when her body softened despite wanting her to wait, but she continued to move as if she hadn't gotten hers off. For her the reason was simple as to why she continued to fuck him hard. There was no knowing if this would happen again or not. So she wanted him to remember a part of why he chose her in the past.

In the hopes that he would choose her again.

"Fuck! You feel so good." He said.

"Don't stop...stay inside of me forever." She said continuing to push back into him. "Please don't go."

He bucked one more time and pulled out before squirting on her back. Lying on the side of her, he looked up at the ceiling, mostly out of breath.

"Walid..."

"Yes." He breathed heavily.

"Can we start all over again?"

Silence.

"I have plans for us." She begged, wiping her long hair out of her eyes. "Things I can do to prove to you that I will never choose something over you again."

Silence.

He sat up, got out of the bed, and walked to her bathroom. From the doorway she could see him washing himself clean of her juices. And she wondered if that meant it would be as if she never existed.

"Walid."

He looked down and back at her on the way to the door.

"Please say something."

"I'm going to keep it straight with you." He fixed his pants.

Her heart rocked. "I'm listening."

"The pussy is still wet. Tight. And clean. I like that about you. But I can't be with you again."

"Why?"

"Because I still don't trust you."

He walked out the door.

She curled up in a ball and started crying.

CHAPTER TWENTY-THREE
UNLIKELY SEPARATION

Spacey was sitting in Sugar's room talking to Minnesota.

It was clear he wanted to rap about the problems of the world.

But she didn't want to talk about anything that would bring Sugar negative energy. Although the little girl still had her bubbly personality, it was taken down a notch since her arm was broken.

And at the moment Spacey looked as if he was going to bring more bad news.

"What's going on with you? Because I can tell something is on your mind."

"He's leaving." He whispered. "He wouldn't even talk about it. Or tell me why."

"Who?"

"Mason."

Her belly bubbled. "What is he leaving for? Is it because of the fight? Because they go at it all the time!"

He looked behind him at the door and back at her. "Don't talk so loudly. You'll wake up Sugar."

She moved closer. "Are you sure though?"

"Yeah, nigga!" Spacey snapped. "That's what the fuck I said. Apparently he's doing it for the boys and to watch Roman."

She sighed and tried to be Wales logical. "Based on history I think this is nothing for us to worry about. However, father has been really distant lately. I walked past his office and he's always making another deal. Helping some YouTubers start their app. Meanwhile this falling to shit." She sighed deeply. "At the same time…we gonna be good. We always are."

"This feels different, Minnesota. He looked spent. Like he didn't have anything left. He's rolling back to the States. I have never seen Mason like that before. I mean tell the truth, have you known him to give up so easily?"

"Based on how you're describing the situation I would say no. Mason always had some fight in him." Her eyes darted around the room as she thought about the future. "I don't even know what life would be like without him. I still remember me and Arylndo dipping off from him as kids. So we could be alone. We thought we were being sneaky. Come to find out he always knew where we were."

"You know sometimes I forget you used to date his son."

"You mean Arlyndo?"

"You know what I mean. Y'all used to cause so much havoc together. We were glad when it was finally over. Although I didn't know he would die the way he did."

Flashbacks of him being poisoned entered his mind.

"I'm sitting here trying to think. And to be honest I don't want to imagine life without Mason."

"You know what's funny." He looked toward her. "All this time we thought Ace would be the one destroying our family and he's nowhere to be found. At the end of the day, pops burning down shit on his own."

"Facts." She sighed. "Joey know yet?"

"Not unless Mason told him." He scratched his neck. "And it looks like he's trying to bounce without anybody knowing. So if I put any bet on it, I would probably say he will want to fly out by the end of the week." He rubbed the back of his head.

"Who taking him?"

His arms dropped at his sides. "He asked me."

She shook her head. "Father is going to be devastated."

"Well let me bounce. Shit too depressing around here. I got this female who's supposed to be coming over later to suck my dick. And I'ma need that shit."

"Spacey, when are you going to settle down? It seems like you been nonstop since you stopped fucking that regular girl who—"

"Do you really want me to answer that question?"

She looked at him for a bit longer. "After all this time you still feel that way? About me?"

He looked at her once more, knocked on the door and left.

Blakeslee was drinking wine and enjoying Mason's company in an Italian restaurant off the island in a quaint town in Belize. The legal drinking age in Belize was eighteen, but it would not have mattered.

They did what they wanted.

Despite her youth, speaking to her was easy.

He was telling her about the stories of when he met Banks as a child. To be honest had he thought about staying on the island and not leaving, he would have never told her the tales.

But if Mason knew nothing else, he knew he had all intentions on leaving within a couple of days. With his bloodline in tow.

"I can't believe y'all used to get in so much trouble as kids." She sighed.

"It's true. We caused a lot of havoc on the streets." He sipped his drink. "But tell me about your boyfriend."

"Who? Fernanda's son?" She frowned.

"I don't know. Is that him?"

She looked down and back at him. "I think that's the one you're talking about. That I brought over to meet everyone." She wiped her hair out of her face. "For some reason, men don't tend to stay around me long. I don't really understand why but…"

"What?"

"If I think about it enough it hurts. So I don't."

He nodded. "Is there somebody that you want and can't have?"

She looked at him and then looked away.

That was an odd question. "There was this other guy who was off island of course. And we were spending a lot of time together after *the crush.*"

"The crush?"

"You know. Sex. The crush." She repeated.

"I must be getting old because I never heard it said like that before."

"So we crushed, and I was happy that the next day he called me. The only reason I didn't call him first was because I was tired, and my phone wasn't charged."

"So normally you are the first person that picks up the phone after sex?"

"Yeah. I mean, I heard that it's good to wait but it never seems to work for me. So I always call within hours, so they won't forget me. But this time I wasn't able to call him back. But when I charged my phone, I had several missed calls from him. He said he wanted to see me again and for the first time in a long time I got excited."

"So I take it that something happened."

"I found out he had a girlfriend in the craziest way. We were over at his aunt's house eating dinner and his uncle who always had too much to drink came out and said `your girl wants to know if you got any money from her yet'."

"Wow."

"Exactly. At first I didn't even think they were talking about me until I saw the look on his face."

"What kind of look was it?"

"Embarrassment. Anyway, he had a girlfriend and a baby the entire time and they were kind of using me for a come up. I was nothing more or less than a few bucks. Still hurts for real."

"I know how it feels not to be wanted."

"Who wouldn't want you? You are everything."

He sat back. "Not everyone feels that way."

"I do."

"Go 'head with that shit." He paused. "Anyway, you have a good life. Once you bypass the people who trying to do you harm you'll see."

"If it's such a good life, why are you leaving?"

"You know, Patrick should not have told you that."

"I never said it was him."

He wiped his mouth with a napkin. "It was that nigga. I know my grandson."

She smiled.

"I'm leaving because there's nothing here for me. I have to start my own foundation. I have to build something for my boys. I got enough money to do that. So it's time for me to go."

She wiped the hair behind her ear, and he could not stop looking at her. Had he thought straight he would have sat on the right or left of her and not directly in front of her face.

Now he was forced to bear witness to her beauty.

To her sexuality.

"Since you're leaving, and I can't convince you to stay, can we spend as much time as possible together?"

"I'm not as interesting as you think."

"I don't believe you. I think you're plenty interesting. And maybe you can spread some of that charm on me."

"I know you're searching for something right now. Banks may be going through whatever he's going through but he'll come around. I know him, Blakeslee. Just give him some time."

"If you know him so much, again, why are you going?"

"Blakeslee, don't ask me that again. Okay?"

"I didn't mean to make you angry. The last thing I need is angering the one person on my side. I'll never bring it up again. I promise. But you're not getting off that easy. You still haven't answered my question. Will you spend more time with me and give me some of your charm?"

"For you, I'll see what I can do."

"To do that it means you have to hang around a little longer."

"Blakeslee…"

"Not telling you to stay…just saying don't leave right now."

"I'll see what I can do."

"That's all a girl can ask. For now anyway."

He chuckled and they drank more wine.

CHAPTER TWENTY-FOUR
BLOOD RED

The moment Walid exited the house after the fuck session, Sydney walked toward Aliyah's room in rage. She allowed her to get her pussy pumped but now she had questions and she demanded answers.

When the door opened, Aliyah jumped up and hid her half-naked body. "What are you doing in here?"

"Can we talk?" She said through clenched teeth.

Aliyah knew it would be hard trying to get her out of her room, so she decided to just give in. "Sit down."

Sydney walked in and flopped on the edge of the bed. "Did I ever tell you about my background?"

"Your background? Do you mean your past?"

"Yes."

"I don't think you gave me a lot but then again, I never really asked. Why do you bring it up now?"

"I helped people with substance-abuse. It was how I met Joey." She laughed softly to herself. "I also was an addict myself for many years. And I saw how hard it was for people to come off the drug. But you know what?"

Silence.

"It's never about the drug, Aliyah. It's always about the inability to deal with the past. To deal with the things that are often too hard to talk about to other people."

"I don't know where you're going."

"Please just listen."

Aliyah nodded.

"When Joey was going through his issues, when he was at his worst stage, he talked a lot. As a matter of fact, he talks so much I don't think he really remembers everything he said to me. But I do."

Aliyah started getting uncomfortable and fixed her clothes while Sydney continued to speak.

"There were days when he was sweating so much and was so sick his mind went into deliria. During these times, he told me about so many things. Like murders. Hidden bodies. And much more."

"Sydney, I don't know what you have planned. But if you're intending in any kind of way to go against the Wales family it would be bad for you. I promise I will get your baby back."

"I'm beyond that now."

"What does that mean?"

"Ace will never give Roman back. Why would he? That's his son. And because of it I have nothing left but secrets. And if I'm going down, I'm taking everyone with me. Banks, Joey, and Mason included."

Aliyah got up and stood in front of her. Decreasing her height she got on her knees and grabbed Sydney's hands. They were cold and clammy but she didn't care.

"I need you to listen to me. If you do what you're about to do and tell anybody about what Joey said to you in confidence things will be bad for you."

"Things are already bad for me now. Look at me."

"They can get plenty worse. The Wales family can touch you any and everywhere. Trust me."

"I said my piece. Did you want anything to drink? Before things do get bad we can at least pretend to be friends."

"O...okay."

Aliyah got up and walked toward the kitchen.

Sydney followed.

Her feet slapping against the cold hardwood floor.

When they made it to the kitchen the first thing they did was turn on the overhead lamp from the microwave. It caused the kitchen to glow without flooding too much lighting that would be sickening or cause headaches.

Sydney poured two glasses of red wine and handed Aliyah one.

Aliyah walked over to her and looked into her eyes. First, she took a sip of her wine and then took a larger gulp. Placing the glass down she stood before her friend with hopeful eyes.

"Please don't do this."

"It's unfair for you to ask me that, Aliyah. Even still I've already made up my mind. I left a message with a detective earlier today."

"But you're getting people involved who have nothing to do with anything. The family doesn't even know Ace is here!"

"You should've given me their numbers so I could tell them."

"I can't do that."

"Maybe. Maybe not. I guess we'll see what happens right?"

Aliyah moved closer to her and while in her grasp, she reached over to the wooden deck and pulled out a butcher knife. Lunging it in her back and torso, she stabbed multiple times until Sydney fell to the floor.

The wine glass in her hand shattered on the ceramic tile.

Aliyah was covered in blood.

Aliyah was covered in shame.

"I'm sorry." She wept looking down at her bludgeoned friend. "I didn't want to do this to you. But you left me no choice. I can't have anything come in between what's going on with my son. I really hope you understand that. And if you don't, I don't give a fuck."

She dropped to her knees and held Sydney in her arms while weeping. When life had washed from her eyes, she called Ace.

"I saw what happened. I'm already on the way."

Ace had taken the body where he needed and returned to Aliyah's house. When he opened the door she was sitting on the sofa with her head hung low. Her fingertips were covered in blood.

"You going to have to get over that shit."

She looked up at him slowly. "How can you be so cold? She may have been dangerous, but she was still a person."

He walked in further and sat across from her on the sofa. "I heard the conversation before you stabbed her. And you were right for doing what you did. Because if you didn't, she was going to blow up your spot and Joey's spot too. To be honest I'm proud of you."

"What I did was nothing to be proud of."

"Depends on who you talking to." He shrugged. "Because you prevented her from rapping to the police. And getting your son snatched."

"She's a liar. She'll say something she doesn't mean just to get a rise. Normally I let it go but this time I couldn't take any chances."

He nodded. "So she wasn't telling the truth? About the cops."

"Probably not. But I guess it doesn't matter anymore, does it? At the end of the day, I pushed off and now I'm going to forever have this over my head."

"Guilt doesn't serve anyone."

Silence.

"On another note, let's talk about that bedroom action. I saw how my brother looked at you. How he responded to you. No matter what he's talking about he misses being in your life. Being in your bed."

"I really wish you wouldn't watch me. I'm getting tired of being viewed."

He laughed. "Why? You a star, girl."

She rolled her eyes. "Cabello, please."

"I love it when you call me that."

She sighed. "If he likes me, why is he fighting me so much?"

"You're the one who got away. And it's always hard to forgive the one who got away. We rich niggas. Rich niggas are hardly ever turned down. And yet you did that shit when you told him it was over. That's something to be proud of."

She didn't see it that way. "So what do you want me to do now?"

"Push him harder. Tell him you're nothing without him. Feed into his ego. Take it as far as possible to the vulnerable side of yourself. Make him feel like you need him to lift you up. Make it like you need him to make you feel like a woman. At some point he will believe you. That shit will sink in his subconscious, and he will literally think that in order for you to breathe he has to do it for you. After that, get him to take you home."

Suddenly the room felt like it was spinning. "So that's what this is about? You want him to take me back to Wales Island?"

"More importantly, I need to know *when* he will take you back to Wales Island."

"You're going to get at Banks and Mason, aren't you?"

"Make him want you again. He already does."

204

"You still sound so sure. How can you be?"

"Because when I look at you, I want to fuck you."

She looked at him harder.

"And if I want to fuck you, that means he wants you back as his wife."

"This is scary."

"It needs to be scary. But we already there. At the finish line. As far as I can tell there's nowhere to go but up. Do you have it in you? To save yourself? To save your son?"

CHAPTER TWENTY-FIVE
THE POTION

Riot paced the beach under the night sky. He was on a mission but needed a little help to push shit off.

When he finally saw Sharon the Shaman, he rushed up to her. "Fuck took you so long?"

She frowned. "You know, I'm getting tired of you and your family acting like I owe you something."

"I'm sorry. It's not like that."

"Then what is it like?"

"Patrick did some grimy ass shit. And I want to get him back."

"Did it have something to do with fucking your girlfriend?" She laughed.

"How did you know?"

"She told me." She giggled. "And she's sad you don't want her anymore. Don't worry, I didn't tell anybody else though. The bitch too stupid to me. Embarrassed Belizeans everywhere."

He glared. "Not worried. Where is it?"

She reached into her purse and handed him a small vial. "All you need is a drop. Place it in his drink. He will be throwing up all night nonstop."

"It won't kill him, will it?"

She grinned. "Let me find out you still have feelings for him."

"Negative. After what he did with my girlfriend, I just don't want him to get sympathy from my grandfather by dying in the house."

"As long as you put only one drop in the drink everything will be fine."

Riot walked into the living room where Sugar was playing a puzzle game with Patrick. She loved individual attention from her family members, and they so truly loved her back.

But Riot wasn't there for Sugar's little hugs and kisses.

He wanted something else.

"Hey, man." Riot was holding two glasses of brown soda.

"Not right now." Patrick warned.

"I'm not beefing with you anymore."

He chuckled. "As if you could ever beef with me."

He was already getting irritated but kept the lie alive. "I'm serious. I'm done arguing with you and I'm done fighting. I want us to drink to new beginnings. Leave all that other stuff behind."

"How convenient." He said as he continued to play with Sugar.

"I'm serious. The last thing we need is to have some female coming in between us. We may not be blood related but we're still family as far as I'm concerned." He extended the drink a little further. "Are we family?"

"We aight."

"Then take a sip."

"Take a sip huh?" He took the cup and put it to his lip. "Is any alcohol in here?"

"No, man. Just soda."

"So you come to me for a truce, and you don't even have liquor in my cup? That doesn't look too good for your position."

"My bad. Didn't want my grandfather or Uncle Mason asking me what I was sipping on so early."

"I hear you. But are you sure you don't have nothing else in here?"

"No." He then took a sip of his own drink as if to convince him. "Now let's drink and cheers."

Patrick looked down at Sugar. "Well, if you don't have any liquor in here I'm sure you don't mind me sharing. You thirsty baby girl?"

Riot felt his stomach drop.

"Yes. I'm thirsty." Sugar said.

Riot came running across the room. "Don't give that to her!"

Patrick glared. "Why?"

"Because she's not supposed to be drinking soda. She just broke her arm. We don't want it to be inflamed."

"It's all right for her to have a sip."

"I said no, man! I don't want her to have any. Now are you going to drink the fucking soda or not?"

Patrick was on to him now and grinned.

"Unless you drink it, I'm going to give it to her." He stood up and walked toward him. "So tell me, Riot, how thirsty are you?"

"Can you just–."

"What you want to do?! Drink it or have me give it to Sugar?"

Still holding his own drink, which wasn't laced with the poison, Riot removed the cup from his hand and took a large sip. Immediately he started feeling weak in the stomach. Within a few more seconds he felt like he was about to explode.

Afraid he would shit on himself; he took off running.

Patrick laughed the whole way.

———✈———

Blakeslee was on cloud nine as she walked down the corridors of the mansion. For starters she was happy that she knew where Ace was at the moment. And since he wasn't on the island, for now anyway, he wouldn't fuck up her plans.

She needed space for a situation she felt was brewing between her and Mason.

In her mind it was time to take it to the next level.

She was walking back toward her room with the cup of coffee in hand when she saw Patrick packing his things. He was grabbing folded shirts and placing them in a box, where other boxes were waiting.

She frowned. "What's going on?"

"Where you been?" Patrick said.

"What you talking about where I been? Why are you packing?" She giggled.

"We moving. I told you that already on the phone."

She assumed after the night she shared with Mason, at the restaurant, that he would change his mind temporarily. They literally sat there for hours talking about the past which quickly merged into the future.

Even though she realized that he was drinking and probably making things up, when she heard him speaking in future tense, she assumed that meant he was staying. Now she was realizing it was all a lie.

"Are you okay?" Patrick said. "Because I didn't know you were this upset about me leaving."

It wasn't hardly about him, but she let him go off.

"I don't understand why he would be moving. Who wants to go back to the States?"

"You have to ask my grandpops. To be honest I don't want to move either. I see how things are going on in America. But there's nothing I can do."

That's exactly what she did.

Went to ask Mason.

When she approached his door, it was locked.

First, she used her hip and when it wouldn't work, she kicked it in instead.

Mason was walking out of the bathroom and was talking on the cell phone when he saw splintered wood on the floor. He had a theory about women crazy enough to kick a door in, but for now he was blind.

"What happened to the door?" He chuckled.

"Sorry…too much pressure."

"Give me a second." He rounded it up with River, his mentee in the States.

For a moment she stood in the open doorway and watched him move back and forth. He was so fucking sexy she wondered why she never saw his swag years ago.

He ended his phone call and approached her with a smile.

A smile that felt different than in the past.

"Hey pretty girl, how your strong ass doing?"

She stepped closer. "What's going on, Mason? Why you leaving right now? I don't….I don't understand."

The smile washed away from his face. "I explained it to you the other night. You had that much to drink that you forgot already?" He tried to grin again, but she was clearly hurt by the news.

"Mason, I'm-."

"Uncle Mason." He said correcting her.

She frowned. "You aren't my uncle. And I know you know that."

He shifted a little.

"I'm begging you not to go."

"You can't do that. It's not fair to me or my boys. I told you that night."

"Why is it that everyone I care about leaves me?"

"You're talking in circles."

"I'm serious!" She said, as tears began to crawl down her face. "If you leave nobody will give a fuck about me."

"That's not true!"

"It is! Think about it. Minnesota has my daughter. Spacey has them both. And my father has a wife. Joey only talks to me in the hallway to tell me to put some clothes on or to get out his face. You were the only one that saw me."

"I'm a grown man! And you shouldn't be attaching yourself that closely to me."

"That's not fair! We-."

"You may be an adult, but you still a child to me! And you need to stay in your place!"

She remained silent, while trembling.

When his cell phone rang again, he picked it up. It was River who was highly concerned. "You good?" She said on the other side.

"I really have to take this." He said firmly to Blakeslee. "Go to your room."

He pushed her out the splintered door and closed it softly.

CHAPTER TWENTY-SIX
BUSY BANKS THE BILLIONAIRE

B anks was in his office going over records for his new business. He spent so much time there that he was starting to let the hair grow out on his face.

Despite his ruggedness, he was still attractive, but it was unlike him not to have every bit of his being in place.

Wanting to talk, Spacey approached the door and Banks looked at him. "It's about time you came to see about me. I called on you yesterday."

"Sorry, I was building Sugar's dollhouse."

Banks sat back in the chair and nodded. "How is she?"

"She's fine." He paused. "Still hugging niggas and giving out kisses and shit."

Banks laughed. "Baby girl is the light for sure."

"Facts." He took a deep breath. "But, uh, can I ask you something?"

He frowned. "What is it, Spacey?"

"Why don't we have breakfast in the morning anymore?"

"You're asking me why we don't do brunch? Because if I recall it was hard getting you there. All of you. Everyone acted like it was a chore."

"That's just young shit, but I see the value in it now."

"I get it. I guess I started realizing you all are adults, and I couldn't push the issue anymore. So I stopped."

"That's what it is? Really? You sure you aren't distracted?"

Banks frowned.

"I mean, how are things, pops? With you."

"I'm good. But I may need you to fly to the States. There's this property that I saw which I want to buy. Before I close on it, I want you to lay eyes on the land."

Spacey nodded.

At one time Banks said they would never return to America but with time and billions made he figured the coast was clear.

"Okay. But that's not what I'm talking about."

Banks sat back in his chair even more. "Then what are you talking about?"

"How are things going with you and Mason?"

His head lowered. "Did Mason's jealous ass send you here?"

"Mason could never be jealous of you!"

"Then what is this about?"

216

"I know how things used to be with both of you. I remember the laughter in the lounge and quiet convos over whiskey. Now on several occasions I caught you both walking past each other without even speaking."

"Stay out of it."

"Can't do that. You made us love Uncle Mason. So, what's going on now?"

He frowned. "You tell me. It's obvious something is on your mind that you want to get off."

"Don't make me remind you. I know about your relationship."

"Spacey..."

"He's your oldest friend. Probably your only friend. Doesn't that stand for something?"

"Mason is getting old."

"And you aren't?"

"Be careful."

"I'm just asking are you getting a little old too? Because to me that's not a reason to not talk to him."

"What I'm trying to say is that he wants things to be his way. And things can't be his way. Not everything. I do a lot for that man. But I think he feels a kind of way for me having a wife."

"I swear I don't think your young wife is it." He said sarcastically.

"I'm telling you it's true."

"Well, I wanted to come to you. Being your oldest son, I figured I could get through to you. Now I see you're stuck in your ways, and I won't push the issue. I just want to say if you really care about your friend you need to tell him. And you need to tell him now." He sighed. "Now I have to check on my son. He been throwing up all day. I think he may be coming down with something."

He walked away.

Mason was pacing the floor of his bedroom.

He felt bad that he went in on Blakeslee and decided to go apologize to smooth things over. But on the way to see her he heard Riot throwing up in his bedroom and he was concerned.

Walking up to his door he knocked once. "You good in there?"

Silence.

The sound of vomit went harder.

"Riot, are you okay?"

"Y...yeah."

Mason entered the room. "What's wrong with you? Why you throwing up?"

"I ate something that made me sick. I'll be fine though. Pops been giving me ginger ale and hot tea." He said holding his stomach. "Seriously, though. I'm fine."

"Do you want me to get the nurse?"

"No! Please don't! I just need a few more minutes."

"Okay. I'll come by and check on you later."

"Thanks, Uncle Mason."

He continued down the hallway to Blakeslee's room. Before entering he took a few moments to get himself together and then knocked once and opened her door.

When he entered, she was crying on the bed on her side.

Concerned, he closed the door behind himself and rushed toward her. "What's wrong, Blakeslee?"

She looked at him and then put her head back into her mattress. "Like you care. Just...just get out."

"Blakeslee, don't do this."

"Don't do what? You told me to leave you alone and that's what I did. Why are you even in my room? It's clear you don't wanna be around me. I can tell when I look in your eyes."

He sat on the edge of the bed. "There's a lot you don't know. And I'm trying to protect you."

She sat up straight and gazed at him. "I'm a woman now. You don't have to protect me." She touched his hand. "But if you can see me...just a little...you'll see I'm the woman who is destined to be your wife."

"Stop talking like-."

"Let's go away...just you and me. I'm begging you."

"You're young and stupid!" He said firmly. "What would you want with an older man? Huh?"

"Please, take me with you."

"Blakeslee...I watched you grow up. I do have to protect-"

Before he could finish his sentence she reached over and kissed him. He tried to push away but it was too passionate.

Too sensual to resist.

"We can't do this." He said despite his dick hardening by the second.

But she wouldn't stop.

Instead she got on his lap and removed his thickness from his pants. Stuffing him inside of her warm vagina she moved softly. The girl was dripping wet.

"I can't be...I can't be doing this to you. It's wrong for-."

"Please don't stop." She kissed him harder. "Please don't come out of me."

He wouldn't be able to pull out if he wanted to at this point. The smell of her pussy was stronger than most but it increased the pheromones in the air.

The woman was real life kryptonite.

Representing the past so much it scared him.

Up until that moment, he thought he was done with wanting Banks as he did back in the day. Now he was realizing Blakeslee represented life as he always hoped it would be when he was in Baltimore.

As he sat tucked in her body, no longer was he an older man.

Now he was a young teenager in love with the love of his life.

"Get this pussy, Mason," she said, with warm breath pushing into his ear. "Get all this pussy, nigga."

His arms wrapped around her waist as he pushed up and into her. "You feel so...so..."

"That's cause I'm yours," she moaned. "Don't you see it? Don't it feel right?"

It did.

"Don't push away your wife," she continued to pop and twerk on his dick. Pussy juice soaked him fully. "You belong to me. I belong to you. Fuck what they think."

Mason was done.

This felt better than he ever could imagine.

Blakeslee, on the other hand, at this moment realized he was obsessed with her. And so she continued to wind her pussy until she exploded on his dick.

Within seconds being unable to control himself he did the same.

Guilt immediately punched him in the face.

It gave him no chance to relish the feeling.

"I got to get up." He tucked himself back into his pants.

"Don't leave, Mason. Please."

"I got to go." He stood up. "I'm so sorry. I should not have taken advantage of you."

"But you-."

"I gotta go." He ran towards the door and rushed out.

Riot stormed into Banks' bedroom where he sat on the bed talking to Faye. He had been sick all night and he was beyond angry at Patrick and 'em.

"Grandfather, can we speak!"

Banks turned toward him. "What's wrong?"

"I have to talk to you."

"You said that already." He quickly got up and walked out of the room with his grandson. The door remained cracked. "Now what is it?"

"I want Patrick and Bolt out of this house."

Banks frowned. "What are you talking about?"

"I want them gone."

"Instead of trying to strong arm me, how about you tell me what the issue is first." He looked at his wife and laughed back at him.

He looked down and back at him. "It's hard to say."

"Let me get this straight you don't have a problem coming into my bedroom and telling me to get rid of family members–"

"Nah!" He scoffed. "But they aren't family members!"

"What are you talking about?"

"They aren't blood. You said it yourself."

"Riot, when did I tell you that Patrick and Bolt weren't family?"

"When we were in the gym. You said that if something were to happen to you or Uncle Mason that they weren't inheritors."

223

Banks was mad busy so the conversation already missed him. He didn't remember the details. "I recall basic information about that night. But let me be clear. Patrick and Bolt are family. And you need to treat them like that."

"Well I won't do it!"

Banks stepped closer and Riot's heart rocked. "What happened?"

Silence.

"Riot, tell me what the fuck happened."

"Patrick messed with my girlfriend."

Banks frowned. "What do you mean, messed with your girlfriend?"

"He was mad because he's not an inheritor. And so he told my girlfriend I wanted to see her and then they had sex."

Banks shook his head. "I don't know what's going on with you and that little girl, but I'll tell you this. The last thing you want to do is let a female come between your relationship."

"I don't get it." He frowned.

"What you mean?"

"You did it with Uncle Mason."

"What are you talking about now?"

"You let Faye come between y'all."

224

Banks looked at the bedroom door and closed it. Although it was too late. Faye heard enough.

Moving closer to him he said, "Riot, I'm grown. Be careful with how you talk to me."

"Sorry, sir."

"I suggest you make good on whatever is going on with Patrick and Bolt. Because at the end of the day they are all you have."

Riot looked as if he wanted to cry.

"What's on your mind now boy?"

"You should take your own advice grandfather." He said before storming away.

CHAPTER TWENTY-SEVEN
REAL GHOSTS

After being out all night, Walid pulled up and parked in front of Aliyah's house. He was about to walk in until his phone rang. "What's up, Spacey? I'm at Baltimore's place. I only got a few minutes."

"Where you at, man?"

Walid's heart dropped. "I just told you. Why you sound all nervous and shit?" Suddenly he got scared. "Wait, that nigga showed up?"

"Who?"

"Ace!"

"Oh, nah. The crazy part is shit is falling down around us and he's nowhere to be found! It's like he said let them kill themselves."

He relaxed in his seat. "Then why you sound all weird? Got my nerves wrecked."

"I think Mason is about to come back to the States. Permanently. Caught him wrapping to River and everything."

He frowned. "I knew he was thinking about coming out here to make sure Ace was not hanging about. But forever?"

"I don't know what's going on with him and pops but it's obvious they aren't seeing eye-to-eye. So he may be coming back to live. And I need you to hurry up and come back to help me fan this shit out before that happens."

It was always something with the family. "Aight, man."

He breathed deeply. "How are my nephews?"

"I haven't seen Roman in a few days."

"Why not?"

"He's always gone."

"That's crazy. He's just a kid. You been there for a couple of days. You don't think anything is up do you?"

"I know I'm not feeling Sydney because she been cringy as fuck. Other than that, I ain't got no comment because my boy good."

"Aight, hurry up back then. Like I said, I need your help."

"Okay....I'll leave in a day."

When Walid ended the call, he walked into the house. Aliyah was standing in the middle of the floor.

"What's up with you? Why you looking all crazy?" He questioned while also gazing around her to be sure no one was about to set him up. Because that was definitely the energy she was giving.

"I want to talk to you, and I just want you to listen." She grasped her own hands tightly.

Silence.

"I want to go back home. To Belize."

He frowned. "Why all of a sudden?"

"Walid, it's not for me anymore to be here. I'm miserable. And have been that way for a long time."

"So you can just pack it up and leave no questions asked?"

"Yes!"

He sat on the sofa with his elbows on his knees. "If you come back to Belize my son has to stay in the mansion. He won't be able to live off the island. I won't feel safe. If I even humor any of this, you have to understand that first."

"I understand."

"Do you? Because there's nothing off the island safe enough for a Wales child. With that said, I can't have you living in the house either. My life is different now."

Her feelings were definitely hurt but she had to continue. "You mean with women?"

"I don't owe you anything."

"I know. I'm only asking because I'm curious."

"I'll say this…I'm a different man from the man you knew. And that's going to have to be good enough. If you return to Belize, which I'm willing to take you, it will not be as a Wales. Or my girl."

Upon the realization that her pussy was weak she said, "Okay…when do we leave?"

———✈———

Blakeslee sat in front of Patrick and Bolt in her bedroom. She seemed off and that made them uncomfortable.

"Well, were you able to do anything to get us to stay?"

She took a deep breath. "No."

"I knew it wouldn't work."

"You sound crazy."

"Seriously. Why would we think that you going to Mason would do anything? It's not like you his girlfriend or something."

Of course they didn't know they had sex. It was embarrassing enough realizing nothing came of it.

She looked down then back at them. "I really don't want y'all to move."

"I thought you didn't even like us." Bolt said.

"I don't. I still don't want y'all getting on my nerves but...I got my reasons for wanting y'all to stay though." She thought about Mason again.

"This house has so many secrets. And it drives me crazy." Patrick said.

She looked at him. "What you talking about? You know something that I don't? Because if you do you need to spill it."

"I just feel like everybody here is always hiding something."

"I'm confused on what this got to do with y'all moving back to the States."

"Yesterday I overheard Uncle Banks talking to Faye. She seemed to be upset about something Riot said."

"She talks to Riot?"

He shrugged. "I don't think so."

She nodded "Speaking of Riot, I haven't seen the three of y'all together. What's up with that?"

"That's cause the Triad is now a duo." Patrick said.

"Stop trying to make that a thing. The duo shit." Bolt said. "I told you it wasn't going to work."

Blakeslee laughed.

"Anyway, she wanted to know about the relationship that Banks and grandpop had with one another back in the day. It was like she was asking for the first time."

"I think we should use the Shaman." She blurted out.

"You mean Sharon's dusty ass?" Patrick pressed.

"Yeah…she be making shit happen."

He stared at her sideways. "You think her spell's going to work?"

"Actually I do. I don't know how she does the things that she does, but I heard she looked out for a lot of people who needed her on the island."

"Apparently she has poison too." Patrick said.

"What you talking about?"

"Your boy Riot tried to poison me."

Blakeslee fell out laughing. "I don't believe you. Riot wouldn't go there. Unless it has something to do with his girlfriend."

"It did." He looked down in shame.

"How you find out he was about to trap you?"

"He came into the living room with some soda. And I saw how he was acting. I said I was going to give it to Sugar–"

"You were going to poison my daughter?"

"You mean Minnesota's daughter."

Blakeslee glared.

"I'm playing. And no, I wasn't going to give it to her for real. But I wanted to see how far he would go. And instead of me faking like I was gonna give it to Sugar, he drank what was in the cup instead. He's been shitting ever since."

"That's what I'm trying to tell you all. She knows how to get things done. But we going to have to give her what she wants."

"What's that?"

"Minnesota's dog."

CHAPTER TWENTY-EIGHT
TAINTED SAND

Banks rolled over and kissed Faye on the cheek. He couldn't get over how beautiful she was, and at the same time, there wasn't any real level to their marriage. For him, foreplay only occurred when they signed multi-million-dollar deals.

However, he still wanted more.

She was getting boring.

When his phone rang, he picked up the call and answered. "Who is this?"

"My family has to leave our house today." It was a female voice, and she was heavily accented. "We can't afford the land and maintenance. And I...I don't know what I'm going to do."

He sat up straight. "Who is this?"

"Kordell's wife."

"How did you get my number?"

"I found Kordell's phone."

He stood up. "And why are you calling me again?"

"What you did when I came to your house was disrespectful. And I didn't think that was in your nature."

"I guess you don't know me."

"I came to you in need, and you ignored me. I thought you were a family man. But that couldn't be the furthest from the truth. I mean, what kind of person would do that?"

"I paid your husband to do a job and he failed."

"But that had nothing to do with me and my kids. Then again, you're known for that. Taking people away from their kids."

"Let me do you a favor–"

"No, you won't do me a favor." She said cutting him off. "What you will do is listen to me. I remember seeing your son when he was here. Long wild dirty hair. Soiled clothing. And even though I didn't know who he was at the time I treated him as a human being. And you never did that for me or mine."

Banks walked over to his window and looked out at the ocean and palm trees dancing in the wind.

Rain had yet to come, and the land was dry.

"And that was a mistake."

"I hope you aren't intending on threatening me."

"No. I don't need to threaten you. If I know the law of the universe, you're already getting the things that you deserve even though you don't see them coming. I don't know where your son is, but I guarantee he has some unfinished business with you. And I wish him all the luck in the world."

"Do yourself a favor and stay in your place before I bury you, bitch."

She laughed and hung up.

Banks grabbed his robe and walked down the hallway. He wanted to get a cold glass of coffee. He preferred it over ice when the weather was extra warm and today was no exception.

Although he tried to put her out of his mind, what she said reigned in his heart.

If he thought about Ace long enough, he would realize that was one of the reasons why he had trouble being with his family. The guilt from how he did Ace was always waiting.

And he wasn't prepared to face it.

Did he do the right thing by giving him to Kordell?

Even though he felt getting rid of him saved lives.

He was almost to the kitchen when he saw several men with boxes moving in the direction of the front door.

"Hold up, who are you?" He glared.

One of them looked at him and walked away.

Irritated, Banks ran up to him and grabbed his arm. "I said who are you? And why are you in my house?"

"We're moving men. We're helping Mr. Louisville move out."

Banks stepped back, and his jaw hung low.

Ace and Arbella just finished making love and he was in such a good mood. Despite not being anywhere near the island, it was obvious that he felt things were going in his favor.

"That dick was good." She said.

"Isn't it always?"

"Not lately."

He chuckled and grabbed a piece of tissue to wipe himself clean. "Well that's about to get a lot better."

"I hope so."

His phone dinged with a text message.

I'm here.

He started texting back because the number was unknown.

Who is this?

It's Aliyah. Your ex-girlfriend.

He looked at Arbella who was glaring having read the words.

"Leave it alone."

She jumped out of the bed and took a shower.

Walking to the door he rushed down the stairs and outside.

Aliyah was in front of the house pacing like a bull.

"Wait...what are you doing with your hair?" She noticed more golden bleached streaks and a strange way he walked.

"Fuck all that. What's going on with you? Do you realize how much trouble you could cause for me around here? By calling yourself my ex-girlfriend."

"I need my son."

"Not until I get what I want."

"I'm doing what you asked."

"Is that why you took the cameras out of the house? Because you're doing what I asked. You think you're smarter than me but you're not."

"I wasn't trying to hide anything. Just didn't feel comfortable with knowing somebody was watching me all hours of the night. So I destroyed them."

He stared harder. "The problem I have with the whole situation is that I thought you and I would be closer. Considering we got rid of a body together and everything. If that's not the case then…"

"I didn't do that because I'm some sort of villain."

"Says every villain everywhere."

"Ace, I need my son."

"Not until I get a confirmation that he's going to take you back to Belize."

"He is going to take me!"

"I need a *when*."

"This is so hard for me." She started crying. "I don't like being this person. Since you came back into the picture everything has changed. You have my son. My friend is dead. It's just so much going on. Why don't you just do what you got to do directly. Why do you have to involve me and my child?"

"Let's not act like that child doesn't have my blood in his veins."

"That's even more reason for you to think about what you're doing."

"Think about what I'm doing?" He said through clenched teeth and walked in her direction.

She stepped back.

He stepped closer. "I thought about what I've been doing for years. You don't know what I went through. You can't even imagine. If you did you wouldn't be so self-serving. Like I told you, I'm not giving you back Baltimore until I get that itinerary. So if I were you, I would get to work." He walked back into the house.

CHAPTER TWENTY-NINE
STORMS

Banks walked past the entrance of his home where Mason's boxes were stacked up high and ready to be boarded onto Spacey's jet. He couldn't believe what he was seeing, and more importantly he couldn't understand why.

Mason was on the beach, directing the movers to pack his things into waiting vans on the carport. The destination was the United States Of Fucking America.

Some place he said he would never return to live.

Walking up to Mason while looking at the boxes disappear before his eyes, he said, "What the fuck is going on?"

Mason looked at him calmly. "What you mean?"

"I don't get what the fuck all this shit is about."

"Why you yelling, man? Ain't nobody but me and you right here." He paused. "So if you wanna talk, try lowering your voice."

Banks was in his feelings, but he was too arrogant to let him know. So he went the old Banks Wales way. Where he felt as if someone owed him their lives and was in no place to ever leave him.

"What's going on with all these boxes around my house? You got strangers coming and going and shit. You know how I am about my privacy. What the fuck is all of this?"

"I'm moving out."

Banks stepped back but stepped forward again.

This was not what he was expecting.

With a scowl on his face. "So, you putting stuff in my hallways and on my beach without giving me notice? After all I did for you?"

Mason looked down and it was obvious he was hurt by his response. "I tried to talk to you several times. But you didn't want to speak. Even called me jealous. So I went ahead and got prepared for the trip. Figured I have to do me."

"This doesn't even make any sense. It's unprofessional."

Mason chuckled. "We've been friends all our lives and unprofessional is the word you choose with me?"

"I mean you're acting like a child."

He nodded. "You're right. I could have gone about this another way. But I'm trying to give you–"

"If somebody saves your life the least you could do is give them the courtesy of telling them you're going back into that space again!"

"Saved my life?"

"Did I use the wrong words? If it wasn't for me, you would still be in that wheelchair living with a wife who beat your ass every night. Not even walking! I paid the doctors to make that happen. You mobile because of my grace."

"Wow. Never thought I would hear you throw that up in my face."

"It's facts."

"Whether you believe it's facts or not I would have never thrown that up in your face if the shoe was on the other foot."

Banks looked away and back at him.

"But like I said, you're right. I should have done my best to tell you I was leaving. Maybe yell at you in the hallway since you didn't want to give me the time when I tried to have a meeting. The good part about it is you never have to worry about me again. Me and my boys are leaving."

"Wait, you're taking Patrick and Bolt too?"

Mason frowned. "Yes. Why would I leave them?"

"Because they have a plush ass life here. Did you even stop to see what it was they wanted? This is crazy. And impulsive. Just like the old Mason Louisville."

"Listen, man, I need to set up a life for my boys. I have enough money to do that. But I can't multiply it the way I want too here. This is a beautiful place. But I have to go back to what I know. Maybe take a few of the pointers I learned from you."

"So you going to sell drugs again?"

"I'm too old for that shit."

"Then what you going to do in the States?"

"Banks, why you asking me all these questions? We don't owe each other anything remember? But if I were you, I would spend more time trying to find out what's going on with our son. Because I haven't moved off my position. I believe he's here."

"So that's what this is about."

"I'm confused."

"You're leaving because of Ace. Okay if that's what you want then I'll put out a search party for him in Mexico. That way you can get out of your fucking feelings and stop acting like a bitch."

Mason laughed and took a deep breath. "I know you're hurting, man. But with time like you do all other things you'll forget about this conversation and me too. I do want you to know that I appreciate everything you've ever done for me. You are right about that. You saved my life. Had it not been for you I don't know where I would be. I'm not just talking about my ex-wife. I'm talking about showing me a better lifestyle. I'm talking about saving me from the streets of Baltimore. I owe everything to you. And I will never ever forget that."

Banks took a step back and looked down.

This shit hurt!

Bad.

Everything in his spirit wanted to beg him to stay. Instead of being vulnerable he said, "Just let me know when you're gone. So I can have my place cleaned properly. Because with all this back and forth, you and them dusty ass niggas making a fucking mess."

He stormed off.

Leaving Mason alone.

Aliyah was sitting on the sofa drinking wine glass after wine glass. She knew Walid would be over soon, but she didn't know how to tell him his son wasn't there. Since he said specifically he was coming to check on him.

Also, she needed a stone confirmation when they were leaving.

And if she didn't have that confirmation Ace would not turn over her child.

When the door opened Aliyah stood up and gripped her hands.

He frowned. "What's up?"

"When are we leaving?"

He walked deeper inside. "Fuck wrong with you? I haven't given you a confirmation yet."

"Walid, I wanna go home. Please. I know you don't want me, but I did share my body with you. I at least deserve an answer."

He sighed. "Okay…in a few days."

"I need an exact date."

"Why?"

"Because I'm sick of being around here."

He nodded slowly; his eyes penetrated hers. "I haven't seen Roman in a while."

She nodded, surprised he was skipping the subject.

"Where is he? Where is Sydney?"

"Walid, I don't know."

"Then why does it look like you're about to pass out, Aliyah? I've known you for a long time. We spent many

245

days together. And I know stress when I see it. Talk to me before I hurt your feelings."

"Ever since you and I broke up I haven't been right. I barely get any sleep. I know it seems that I've been having things under control, but it took a lot for me to finally tell you how I feel. And now that I've told you my feelings they are rushing out at quick speeds. I dream of going back home. So now that I know that I am, I fear that it will be taken away."

"I don't believe you. Where is Sydney? Where is Roman?"

"I don't know, Walid! She's a grown woman. They could be anywhere."

He stepped even closer.

He was so close this time she could not move. "Well where is my son?"

"He's…. he's…"

"He's where?!"

"Over a friend's house. I was going to get him, but I thought you weren't coming until later. And I wanted to spend this time talking to you first. I'm sorry."

"I want you to go get him."

"Why can't he stay with his friend?"

"Aliyah, don't make me hurt you. Go get my fucking son! Now!"

Fifteen minutes later, Aliyah was back at the ho house. At first she was afraid Ace wasn't going to open the door but luckily he was sitting on the front porch of the brothel talking to Arbella.

They were sharing cold glasses of spiked iced tea and Ace had a large gauze patch on his chest.

Jumping out of the car with the door swinging open she said, "He says we leaving tomorrow." She was lying but she didn't care.

"How do I know I can believe you?"

"Ace, this is the most traumatic thing I've ever experienced in my life. And I'm not asking for sympathy. But I'm telling you that I did everything that you wanted. Now he wants his son."

"Please don't act like you didn't want the man back anyway." Arbella said. "If anything he did you a favor by forcing what you already desired."

Aliyah was shocked she spoke to her directly because she hardly ever did. Usually all she had for her was eye-rolling and heavy sighs. So the fact that she was opening her mouth now was different.

247

"Are you really going to talk to me about my boyfriend? The nigga you fucked because you didn't know your own man's dick! Is that what we're doing tonight?"

Arbella was so embarrassed she fell backwards before sitting back up again. One thing that was always off limits in her world and was not open for discussion, was the fact that she slept with Walid.

Even though it was under the guise of believing it was Ace, Ace never got over this detail.

"Don't forget I have your son," Arbella said. "In case you need remembering."

"Touch my son and I'll kill you, bitch," Aliyah announced.

"That dick must be doing you right in Bowie." Ace said through clenched teeth. "Because you have a mouth on you tonight don't you?"

Aliyah calmed down upon hearing his voice. "Ace, I didn't mean to be disrespectful. But like I said this has all been traumatic. And the last thing I need is someone pointing fingers my way."

He nodded. "Tomorrow huh?"

"Yes. What you going to do when we leave?"

"Are you sure you want to know? Because if I tell you any of my plans, life as you know it would be over."

She shook her head quickly from right to left. "No, don't tell me."

"So it's settled."

"I need my son."

"I forgot about that already. What do you need him for?"

"He threatened my life if I didn't bring Baltimore back."

"So…" He shrugged.

"Ace, you know your brother more than me. At one point I thought it wasn't possible for two people to know so much about the other even though time has passed."

He smiled.

"But let's not play any games. There is no way on planet Earth that your brother is going to leave without his child. Or allow me to come home without him. Please give him to me. And do whatever you gotta do short of hurting us."

He chuckled and looked over at Arbella. "Go get nephew."

Arbella slowly got up, looked at Aliyah, rolled her eyes, and walked into the house.

"That was something else." Ace said, sipping his drink.

"What are you talking about?"

"How you came at my girl."

"She was in the wrong."

"Unfortunately for you, her memory is long. I'm just letting you know in advance."

CHAPTER THIRTY
IN A WALID MINUTE

Aliyah had no idea Walid would be pulling out that night to go back to Belize. Shit moved so quickly she didn't have time to breathe.

The moment she pulled up in front of her house, it was surrounded by armed security.

"We leaving tonight," Walid said plainly.

"But I thought you said in a few days."

"Tonight."

Thirty minutes later, they were on the road. He told her outside of her government documents to leave all else. He would buy her a whole new wardrobe.

Just like that she was on her way home.

He was driving down the highway quickly on the way to his plane. Two cars filled with security tailed behind the billionaire. He learned from his father never to be caught slipping particularly when he was getting ready to go back home.

When he glanced over at Aliyah, he noticed she was trembling. "You're getting what you want. So, what's up with you now? Why aren't you happy?"

She looked at him and swallowed the lump forming in her throat.

"Answer me, Aliyah."

"I…I have to tell you something and I don't know how to say it."

"My brother is in town."

Her headshot in his direction. "How did you know?"

"I knew for sure tonight. And after not seeing Roman for days in a row. Even though Sydney was Joey's ex-wife, that's still his son and I can't see him letting her keep him forever. I figured he snatched him after that."

"I'm so sorry. I hated lying to you."

"So everything that you said to me was false?"

She believed he was talking about the fact that she wanted to be with him. And she needed him to know that everything she said about missing him was true.

"Not everything was a lie."

He looked in the back seat at his son who was asleep and then back at her. "What part was real? I'm asking for a friend."

She looked down and took a deep breath. "I truly want to get back with you. I made a mistake."

"When did you figure that out? When my brother came back?"

"I knew before then. Was too afraid to let you know."

He dragged a hand down his face and continued to steer the car. "I figured he would come back and start trouble. To be honest I didn't think it would be this soon. But I knew at some point he would return."

"And you still allowed me to live here with Baltimore?"

"Not really."

"I don't understand."

"When I got news that he was no longer in Mexico I realized letting Baltimore stay here was not going to be a thing. Not for me anyway. My plan was just to take my son back on this trip and leave you to it, in the States. I made arrangements here and on Wales Island to set my son up for greatness."

Her eyes widened. "I would have died without my baby. Sometimes I speak to Riot's mother and I can't get over how sad she is. The hardest thing ever is to not be with your child. I can't believe you were going to do that to me."

"I don't know why you're surprised. I always told you he would remain here as long as I felt he was safe. And shit ain't safe no more."

"So it's a good thing I asked to come back with you."

He made a right. "Basically."

"I can't believe this shit! Ace coming back was the only thing that allowed me to be with my son."

His brows lowered. "What did my brother say he was up to?"

"That's just it, he didn't tell me anything. He showed up in the middle of the night. At one point he had my house bugged until I removed the cameras. His only goal was to get me to get back with you."

"That's not his only goal. Trust me."

"Well that's all he told me."

"He doesn't have any money, so I'm still not concerned."

One thing Aliyah didn't share with him was that he was in possession of Baltimore's stipend card. Which at last count had $167,000 on it.

He had stolen it from her, and she would take that mishap to her grave.

Fifteen minutes later, Walid pulled up to the hangar and parked his car.

The armed men following exited their vehicles and made sure he was protected. After a few signatures, which included red tape for him to be able to fly were done, he was escorted to his plane.

It took a moment but soon they were up in the air and still she felt uneasy. Looking around as if Ace would pull alongside the jet and shoot it down.

Picking up his phone, Walid dialed the number. "Pops."

Mason was exhausted. "Yes, son."

"You were right. Ace is here."

"Did you see him?" He said anxiously.

"No. But I'm on my way back with Aliyah and Baltimore."

"Good decision. What about my other grandson? What about Roman?"

He looked at Aliyah and back at the skyline. "He wasn't there. But I'll come back for him later."

"Don't you worry about anything. I have it from here. I'm moving back to the States."

"I heard. Hopefully we can talk later. Because I want you with me, pops. Please."

"Don't worry yourself, son. No matter what, we're good."

CHAPTER THIRTY-ONE
FAMILY FIRST

Riot was in his room trying to find a new girlfriend. Ever since he saw the video with Patrick, he was done with the old chick. And ready to move on to the next thing. And then Mason entered the room.

"Got a minute?" Mason asked.

"Yes, sir."

Mason walked inside. "I heard about what happened between you and Patrick. And I want to say I'm sorry about that. I liked that girl for you."

Riot looked down. "Me too."

"Did you tell your father?"

"No...I don't want him mad."

Mason nodded. "I want to tell you something you may not know. When you grow up together as teenagers that kind of thing happens all the time. But there is no reason to destroy the bond."

"That was my only girlfriend though."

Mason chuckled. "I know, man. I get it. But there will be plenty of women in your life. Me and your grandfather been through it all, wives included, and we remain friends."

He nodded.

"I will say this, you were right for setting Patrick straight. Never move off your morals. But just remember that at the end of the day, family is everything."

Riot took a deep breath and looked up at him. "Please don't go. Please don't take them with you. I won't have anybody else my age here."

Mason smiled. "So you heard too?"

"Yes. Saw the bags and boxes."

It felt good that he got so serious about how important it was to have a family.

"I have to leave. But I came in here because I want you to know that I get how you were feeling. And we will connect again. All of us."

They hugged and he walked out.

After Mason finished with Riot, he went to Patrick and Bolt who were moping around in Patrick's room due to leaving for the States later that night. It was last minute, which shocked them because Mason gave no notice. He put on as if they had more time.

Now after hearing about Ace he was in a rush.

"Okay, are you all packed?" Mason continued. "Because I don't wanna be delayed. I think a windstorm is supposed to be coming later."

"Yes." Patrick said with a deep breath.

"You finished packing too?" He looked at Bolt.

"Yes, father."

"Good. Now go see Riot. Make amends. I don't want us to leave with things being bad between you three."

To be honest they wanted to end the beef anyway. But they were looking for someone to force them just like Mason was doing now.

"Alright. I guess I'll talk to the nigga." Patrick sighed as he and Bolt moved toward the door. Once in the hallway he said, "Oh, Uncle Banks wants to speak to you. He's in the boardroom I think."

Mason frowned. "Did he say what he wanted to speak about?"

"No."

"Aight...thanks."

Confused, Mason trudged to the boardroom.

It was a room that Banks created for Faye and him to make multimillion dollar business deals. Usually, it was off limits to everyone else.

But tonight, when he walked inside, he was surprised at the ambiance. The recessed lights were slightly dim and were only on over the boardroom table which made the mahogany surface look like extra wet honey.

Music always played in the mansion during certain hours. And those who didn't want the music simply cut the speakers off in their room.

But right now, they were playing a specific song.

Never Felt This Way by Brian McKnight.

"There will never come a day…you'll ever hear me say…"

Banks was seated on one end of the table and had a stack of papers in front of him. Mason stood on the opposite end of the table and had a stack of papers in front of him too.

"Have a seat man." Banks said, seriously. His diamond chain sparkled like the bracelet on his wrist. "Please."

He looked down at the papers and back at him. "What is this about?"

"Please sit down."

Mason rolled his eyes, sat down and briefly eyed the documents in front of him.

Banks took a deep breath. It was long and hard, but he needed it to say what he was about to say next. "I have been playing over in my mind what would make you want to leave. To be honest I haven't really been thinking straight since you told me."

"I'm sorry to hear that, man." He said honestly.

"Me too. Because my absent-mindedness is the cause of one of the most important people in my life not feeling me. At first, I didn't know where my mind was. Like where my thoughts went. And anytime somebody brought up Ace I chose not to hear it. But everything I've built was for my family. Ace included. And it hurt when he didn't receive what I was building."

"You know I know that, man."

"I know, but I still need to say this. When I had my vision for this island, I didn't think about us as men. With two families. We aren't kids anymore. People depend on us."

"You know you're closer to a brother to me. We gonna always be two niggas from Baltimore, city. Different last names or not."

"That may be true. Actually, it is true. But you do have a bloodline. You do need to make sure things are set up when you die. And if I was a real friend, I would have thought about that before now."

"Man, you looked out for me by putting money in an account I could draw from."

"You and I both know based on the lifestyle we live; millions don't last long. But what I'm about to do today will be forever." He nodded his head at one of the men who hung at the wall. He walked over and gave Mason a blue ballpoint pen.

"What is this?"

"I'm giving you half of Wales Industries."

Mason's eyes widened. "What are you talking about? There are billions in your accounts."

"I guess that makes you and your family billionaires too. Now sign the documents."

Mason had lived a long time.

And there have been a lot of gestures done in his honor. But none of them made him a billionaire. None of them put him in a position to take care of his family and his family's family, until now.

Banks was not only saying that he heard him loud and clearly, but he was also saying that at the end of the day the money didn't matter if their friendship wasn't intact.

And Mason loved him even harder for it.

But what about Blakeslee?

And the things he'd done with her, due to lust?

He actually fucked his best friend's daughter!

Where was the honor in that shit?

And what about the fact that, even now, he would always hold onto the love he had for the girl back in Baltimore even though she was long gone?

261

"I got to tell you something."

"To be honest, Mason, I don't want to hear nothing that's going to destroy this deal. Please sign it. Let me take care of you and your family. Scratch that. Let me put you in a position to take care of you and your family so that we can be one."

"What God has joined together let no man tear apart," Mason said.

"Without first catching a bullet," Banks ended. "Now sign the mothafuckin' papers."

Mason hadn't cried in years. And yet as he was signing the documents that would make him a billionaire tears dropped on the papers.

When he was done the gentlemen grabbed the documents to solidify the transaction.

Banks smiled at him from down the other end. "Now get your boxes off my beach and put them back in the house. You fucking up the sand."

Mason broke out into heavy laughter that quieted slowly.

"Now, let's talk about our son. I was right, Banks. He's back."

CHAPTER THIRTY-TWO
SWEET PUSSY

Minnesota was playing with Sugar in her room. She appreciated her high energy despite wearing a cast on her arm after all she'd been through. It was good hanging around an innocent child who kept her all kinds of busy. Also, since Minnesota didn't know what was going on with Mason and Banks she needed to stay in an upbeat mood.

When Sugar jumped off the bed and did a superman run toward the middle of the room, she said, "Sugar, you're going to tire yourself out."

Instead of listening she laughed and took off running down the hallway. The unbound arm swinging rapidly. Concerned, Minnesota went running behind her, for fear she would get hurt.

Despite being chased, Sugar saw no signs of slowing down. Instead, she sprinted down the hallway and laughed in the contagious way babies did which caused her to giggle too.

Before she knew it they ended up in Blakeslee's room.

Just like herself, Blakeslee hated people in her personal space. And Minnesota would not have gone inside had her niece not entered.

But there she was, violating her privacy by walking into her room.

"Sugar, let's get out of here. I don't want to hear Blakeslee's mouth." She scooped her up when suddenly she saw her dog's toy on the side of the bed. Placing Sugar back on her feet she grabbed the toy and looked at it.

"Hold up, what is this doing in here?"

Now even more curious, she started looking around from where she stood. Next to her bed was an open dresser drawer. She pulled it slightly and saw what appeared to be a journal.

It was a new age type.

All digital.

She would have thought it was an iPad, but it literally had the word *journal* etched into the steel above the screen. There was no way she would walk out without satisfying her nosiness.

"This can't be open." Minnesota said to herself as Sugar continued to run around the room. "She has to have a password on it."

She tapped it once and Blakeslee's face appeared on the wallpaper. Sliding her finger to the right, Blakeslee's latest journal entry popped open before her eyes.

"It is unlocked. Girl, are you crazy?"

Curious and nosy at the same time, she sat on the edge of the soft bed and read the entry. What she took in literally snatched her breath away.

Blakeslee spoke about her obsession with Mason and her urge for power. She spoke about how they enjoyed each other's company while going out to eat.

But it was the final entry that shook her.

She went into detail about how it felt to fuck Mason. How the anxiety of the moment heightened her orgasm.

What scared her the most, was her plan to be Mason's wife.

Blakeslee was definitely a troublemaker, and she did allow lies to flop out of her mouth every now and again. But Minnesota couldn't imagine what would possess her to put such vicious lies in her personal diary.

And then she realized it wasn't a lie.

It was the truth.

Everyone knew Blakeslee reminded him of Banks as a girl.

Would they run off together?

This was bad for the family for sure.

Holding the journal in her hand she had a couple of choices. She could put it back and risk someone else finding this and destroying a bond between her father and Mason that she'd come to respect and love.

Or she could throw it in the trash.

She snatched Sugar and took the device with her.

The baby giggled hard, as if she knew of things to come.

Aliyah's leg was trembling as she sat in the cockpit with Walid and his co-pilot. He was really grateful he had assistance because she was a nervous wreck and he figured she needed his attention at the moment.

Ordinarily he would ignore her, since she was no longer his girl. But Baltimore was starting to feed off her energy by crying and moaning.

"What is it now, Aliyah? This anxious shit fucking with my son. You need to calm the fuck down."

"I want to say something, but I don't want you scared." She said softly.

"What is it?"

"Did you check this plane? Before we got on? Because I don't understand what his plan is and it's scaring me."

He laughed. "That's all it is?"

"Walid..."

"There is no way that I can fly any plane without checking all around and under it. I done seen too many things in my family. So yes, the coast is clear."

She felt as if a physical weight had been taken off her shoulders.

He took a deep breath. "I don't know where Ace is but he's not on my plane and he's not on the island."

She started crying. "This family feels so overwhelming at times."

"I know. That's how I lost you in the first place."

She looked up at him. It was the first vulnerable thing he said to her since they had broken up. "Nah, that was on me."

"Not really. At first when you broke up with me, I was upset. Took me a long time to get over it. But then I thought about it. Being a Wales is a lot of work. It's a lot of pain. And you kind of made me feel better when you ended it because at least I didn't have to worry about you."

"But it was a mistake. To let you go."

"Was it? Look at you right now. You're distraught because of my twin brother. Things like this are going to always be an issue with my family. I know it in my heart. There's no way around it."

"Yes, I'm scared. But it's mainly because I felt like I was doing it alone. Like I didn't have you."

"I never said we were back together."

"I know that."

"Do you? Because I've built up a life for myself that I don't want ruined. By having to answer to someone."

"Walid, I don't know what you're doing out there in the world. I truly don't. If I know you, you're probably making a lot of women happy." She inhaled and exhaled. "But I do know that I am meant to be your girlfriend. Your wife. And if I have to wait for you to come around then that's exactly what I will do. And there's nothing that you can say that will convince me otherwise."

"Aliyah, I-."

"I dream of us back together again. I dream of us being a family again. And I will see that become reality."

"Do you promise?"

"Do I promise that I want you?"

"Do you promise that you can handle not being my girl?"

"I'm not going to lie and say it won't hurt. I guess that's the good part about me living off the island. At least I won't have to see the women you bring into the mansion."

"Living off island?"

"Yes…you said I couldn't stay at the mansion."

He waved the air. "I'm just fucking with you."

She rubbed her temples. "What part?"

"There's no way I'm taking you back to Belize and putting you in the same conditions I took you out of. You're my son's mother. I just wanted to make sure that you understand that we aren't together. If you can get with that, you're more than welcome to stay with me in the mansion. In your own room. Not in my bed."

"Like how it was when we were younger." She said excitedly.

"I guess."

She smiled and covered her mouth with her trembling hands. "Thank you. Thank you. I just wanna be able to look after my son."

At that moment, they didn't have a care in the world.

The blue skies were their friends.

And in the distance several planes went about their destination. Even one that included his brother Ace and his girlfriend Arbella.

Ace needed to find out when they were leaving not so he could get on their plane.

But so he could have it followed by a seasoned pilot who, using radar and TACACS, respected the laws of wake turbulence by following no closer than 1000 feet behind Walid's plane.

Assuming they were just another plane, Walid would never know.

CHAPTER THIRTY-THREE
OUR WICKED SON

Mason and Banks stood in the lounge drinking whiskey trying to think of all the ways Ace might pose a problem for the family.

And Banks couldn't think of one way.

"Even if he's in the States, I just don't think this is going to be a situation we have to worry about. And I realize how frustrating this is for you. But I know it would be impossible for him to wait two years and not come to see me if he was so angry and had money. Plus, how would he get here? We are literally off the grid."

"You're right on that part. Walid told me he checked his plane before coming back. So he's not there."

"See..." Banks said, believing his point was made.

"He's still probably plotting something HUGE." Mason continued.

"Plotting that long? For two years. You give him that much credit? Because I sure don't."

"Ace is embarrassed, Banks. I'm sure he finally realizes how the moves he made took him right out of the money line. And that anger has to be directed somewhere. And I think it's at us."

271

Banks shook his head. "Not us. Just me."

"If it's you it's me too."

Banks took a deep breath. "So what do you propose we do? Live like he's always around the corner? Nobody is going to allow him on our island unless he connects with one of us. And none of the kids will let him either."

"Are you sure about that?" Mason leaned closer.

"Who you talking about being disloyal? Walid?"

"Of course not. The boy is solid. Besides, Walid wants nothing to do with him. Especially after he made trouble for him and Aliyah. Also, he respects us too much."

"Then who will go against my rules? Because I've made it clear I don't want him anywhere near our island or this Mansion."

Mason was quiet for a moment.

Besides, guilt crept up into his heart. After all, he slept with the person he was most concerned about and was having a hard time telling Banks.

"What about…uh…Blakeslee?"

Banks laughed. "What about her?"

"How do you know she won't betray us…I mean you?"

"I'm going to tell you something you probably don't know about me. I have somebody looking at Blakeslee every time she leaves this island. Because I don't trust her."

Mason felt dizzy.

Although going to dinner with her was innocent enough it later led to something much deeper. Something much more sinister.

Did he know?

"And what does that mean?" He said, folding his arms on his chest.

"The men at the gate know that unless it's her friend, she is not allowed to let anyone access this island without approval. So it can't be her. I'm a hundred percent sure."

"Still, I think we should beef up security."

"I don't have a problem with that."

"I mean like today, Banks."

"Easy, man. We haven't even officially celebrated your billionaire status. And you're more stressed than ever."

"You and I both know money doesn't make all your problems go away."

"Nope, but it sure makes it shinier."

Mason smiled. "It's not easy saying you're afraid of your own son. And yet here I am saying just that. Maybe after it's all said and done I can kick back and realize how blessed I am that you set the Louisville's up for the rest of our lives. But Ace, I just feel off about him. I saw the look in his eyes when we put that hood over his head before shipping him to Mexico. I'm sure he's been thinking about that every day too. And I know when he gets an opportunity to shoot he won't miss. That's really all I'm saying."

"I don't miss either." Banks reminded him. "So if he comes, he better be sure."

Sitting next to Arbella on the jet, Ace was busy with his cell phone.

When Aliyah rushed to get Baltimore, Ace felt Walid was trying to bounce early. So grabbing bags already packed, he and Arbella hit it to the hanger where his paid pilot was ready to fly out, using the money from Baltimore's stipend account.

The fact that he would be in Belize soon got him excited. He dreamed of this night. He dreamed of finally being able to get revenge in his own special way.

And so he sat on the phone trying to get a hold of his associate.

274

Paulo.

A do the dirty work kind of nigga in Belize. Ace had a thing for connecting with the most dangerous, so keeping seedy friends was right in line.

But why wasn't he answering his phone?

His plan had timestamps and deadlines to be met.

"Are you okay?" She asked, rubbing his leg.

He looked at Arbella and took a deep breath. "I'm fine. But there are some things I need to happen."

"Paulo is going to call back."

He tried again. "How can you be sure?"

"You have mentally rehearsed this moment for months in your mind."

"How you know?"

"You recite it in your sleep. And while the world moved on, you kept this image in your mind, and so it will come to pass."

"You sound like you believe in me now."

"I never not believed in you." She wiped her hair out of her face. "I was just afraid of what will happen to us if you get what you want." She grabbed his hand tightly and squeezed. "I'm still scared now. But I will ride with you through it all. Even hell. No matter what."

He kissed her lips.

"But when this is settled, I want Aliyah." She said firmly.

"For what?"

"I got plans for that, bitch," she glared.

He winked and suddenly the phone rang.

He removed his hand from hers and answered.

"You see," she winked back.

He focused on the call. "I've been hitting you all day. Where you been?"

"There's a lot going on. But I'm here now. What's up?"

"I'm in route. And I need to make sure that you have the men necessary for my plan."

"Yes, Cabello. We are ready. Shall I call my sister, Sharon? We already laid down the accelerant."

"I thought you couldn't get in contact with her?"

"I ended up finding her," he sighed. "She was worried about some dog dying in all this shit but she good now."

"Cool." He shook his head. "I'm going to need a ride."

"Already scheduled the moment you land."

"Every one of you is getting ready to be wealthy."

"A rich man in my own country? That's a dream come true."

CHAPTER THIRTY-FOUR
WORRIED WORDS

Minnesota was pacing the floor waiting on Spacey. She was actually in his room because what she had to say she felt needed to be said now.

"Why you looking all crazy?" He said throwing his wallet and keys on his dresser. "And why you in my room?"

"Oh, so now you have a problem with me being in your room?"

"Sometimes I think you're baiting me. Let's not go there."

"You're right. My bad."

"So what you want?"

"I have to tell you something and I don't know how to say it. Before I get started it has nothing to do with you, me, or anybody that we really like in this family. I just want to say that first."

"That leaves Ace."

"Nah."

"Does it have to do with a parent?"

"Nope, not a parent either. Nobody that we like."

277

"Okay I'm going about this the wrong way, who *is* involved? Let's start there. Because already you driving me crazy."

"It's about Blakeslee."

"And who else?"

"Mason."

"But Mason is a parent, and we like him."

"Well, that's true, we do fuck with him. Thinking of the old days. But he's not a parent. Y'all spending too much time together and you're starting to believe he your daddy."

Spacey thought about it for a minute. It wasn't that he thought he was his parent but every now and again it felt like he could possibly have two fathers. Maybe it was the way that Mason was always in the picture or how he looked out for him during some pretty dark times.

Either way he was definitely confused at the moment.

"I know he's not my father, but you know what I'm saying. Now what's going on? Cause you keeping me in suspense."

"I found Blakeslee's digital diary."

"You looked in it?"

"It was open! What else was I supposed to do?"

"Anything but read the girl's shit."

"Spacey, I promise you that's the least of our worries." She flopped on the edge of his bed. "Like I said, it's about Blakeslee and Mason."

"What about them?"

"They had sex."

Spacey laughed.

He was hoping she was telling a joke even though he didn't know her for her comedy. When he saw she wasn't budging he moved closer. Then he walked away and closed the door and moved closer again.

"Are you actually telling me they fucked?"

"Yes."

He placed both hands on the sides of his head. "Why would you even come to me with this? Now you got it in my mind too."

"I had to tell somebody."

"Not really! This the kind of shit you take to your grave!" He said pointing at the ground.

"I just didn't want to know it by myself." She admitted.

"Wow."

"What do we do?" Her eyes fluttered.

"Let's go back to what I said originally. We don't ever speak on it again."

"But why would he do that? Blakeslee is so nasty." She shook her head. "On several occasions I smelled her pussy when she walked by."

"Joey too! He told her to clean that shit when they passed in the hallway one night."

"Damn...Mason want daddy back so bad he fucking a dopplaganger?"

"I spoke to Mason before, over drinks. And several times under his breath he said that she looks exactly how pops would have looked if he was a girl." He shook his head. "He would zone out and I don't even think he knew I was in the room still."

"I heard that before too." She frowned. "I mean, think about when father lost his memory."

"Yeah...he had my nigga in a skirt and everything."

They shuddered remembering Banks' female days.

Suddenly Minnesota's mind wandered.

"Why you looking like that?" He asked.

"Why didn't I get to look like him when he was younger?"

"Hold up, you want to fuck Mason too?"

"Don't be stupid!"

"You're the one who sounds stupid. We got issues going on and you want to know why you don't look like pops when he was a little girl? Like I said we don't speak on this ever again."

He pointed in her face and she slapped his hand away.

"You don't have to worry about me. I'm already mad, I told you."

"Me too!" He paused. "Now let's go find Blakeslee. And threaten her to fucking secrecy."

"Yeah. Also I want to find out where the fuck is my dog."

Blakeslee was in the woods with the Shaman, Patrick, and Bolt.

The Shaman had promised to do a spell that was guaranteed to make Mason stay and not go back to the States. At first they wondered why she wanted to go into the forest right on the outside of the land. She claimed she was looking for a sacred space.

Stopping next to a large brick colored rock she said, "This is perfect."

But before she did anything she wanted to be paid.

As she saw Minnesota's dog tucked under Blakeslee's arm, a smile came to her face. "Hand it here."

"We want to make sure you're able to do this shit first." Patrick said. "No results. No pup."

"I already feel dumb as fuck." Bolt added. "We ain't paying unless we know this shit works."

"Trust me I can do it. Now give me my dog."

Blakeslee took a deep breath and handed her the animal. "What are you going to do? Because to be honest I'm tired of waiting."

She placed the dog on the ground and said, "Stay." For some reason the dog didn't move. As if it were too frightened.

Did it know something they didn't?

Blakeslee looked at Bolt and Patrick in confusion.

Pit-Pat didn't listen to nobody.

Not even Minnesota.

Next Sharon removed a lighter and a bundle of hay from her pocket. She also removed some hair from Mason's brush as well as a piece of tissue he threw in the trash weeks ago.

Putting them together, she made a pile and lit it on fire.

"Fuck is you doing?" Patrick asked.

"My miracle!"

Sharon may have had other reasons for doing her work in the forest, but she took what she did seriously too.

The moment she laid fire, it accelerated like it was lighting up a runway. Starting next to them, it lit up in many different directions in looping manners. Quickly it began to engulf everything in its path. As they looked at the fire blaze, their pupils glowed orange.

"Okay...how big does this gotta be for us to stay on this bitch?" Blakeslee said.

"We should get out of here." Sharon picked up the animal. "Trust me though...it works. Y'all ain't going nowhere."

Unfortunately, where they were, the land was extremely dry and suddenly when a gust of wind came through, pieces of debris took flying fireballs to the air.

Each watched as pieces connected to trees.

"Fuck is y'all...?" Spacey lost his words as he took in the dreaded scene. "Wait...what y'all trying to do? Burn us out!"

"Right!" Minnesota asked. "What is this shit?"

Sharon took off running with the animal in the opposite direction.

Suddenly he and Minnesota started fanning flames and more fire flew everywhere resulting in a full-fledged disaster. Blakeslee, Patrick, and Bolt tried to help but they only made matters worse.

In horror, the five of them could do nothing but watch.

"It's no way to stop it," Minnesota said softly, covering her mouth.

"It's...it's really not." Blakeslee whispered.

Slowly Spacey turned his head and looked at all of them. His back was against the inferno. "We tell no one of this. We say nothing about what happened here."

"I don't even know what happened," Minnesota coughed.

"Sharon started the fire," Patrick blurted out.

"And we all made it worse," Bolt hacked.

"Father will be devastated." Minnesota said, as they all began to back away from the raging flames. "There's no way of getting out of this. He will hate us for life!"

"We'll find a way to clear our names. And we'll know it when we see it."

The night sky was a rich purple...

Golden stars twinkled in every direction as Banks Wales stood on his beach looking at a disaster go down before his eyes. The diamond chain with a modest sized medallion sparkled against his vanilla, bronzed skin which was coated with a thin sheen of sweat due to the heat.

The sexy, salt and pepper, fully tatted up Baltimore native standing on the beach shirtless, was a beautiful contrast to the trees that outlined his property. Because as he continued to look in the distance his eyes flickered orange, due to the blaze eating up the land and brush while also threatening to destroy everything he built.

Wales Island.

His heart was breaking.

His world was shaking.

"What the fuck are you doing out here?!" Mason asked, rushing up to him. His black Versace shirt hung open, showcasing a tennis diamond necklace. "We have to get the family, get on boats and leave!" He looked at the fire which was growing quickly and back at his friend.

Although the devastation also ripped his heart he didn't care as much as Banks at the moment.

"Did you hear me? Let's go!"

Banks wanted to move.

In fact, he wanted nothing more. But his feet seemed to dig deeper into the beach almost as if it were trying to swallow him whole.

This island with its glittering sand was always a dream.

The only thing he wanted more than those nearest and dearest to his heart. And now it was possible that it would be all for nothing.

"Why do things like this keep happening to me?" He turned his head in Mason's direction. "Look at my island."

Mason gazed quickly before refocusing on his friend. Almost as if the land was an afterthought. As if the island were a stranger walking by whose face he wouldn't remember the moment they bounced.

Truth be told he didn't give a fuck.

Let it all burn!

After all, although Mason enjoyed the serenity the land brought them both, nothing meant more to him than the man standing in front of him. And he wanted to ensure that he, their children, and the seeds that followed would be safe.

Banks turned his head toward him. "I can't walk away. Why can't I move?"

286

"Banks, I know this shit is rough! But we have to find our family and bounce! Wake the fuck up! This shit is about to be an inferno."

Banks looked down. "You know I don't complain. I try and keep my head level. But what did I do in my life not to get the dream?"

The man had selective memory, that was certain.

How quickly he'd forgotten about the bodies.

The drug lifestyle which afforded him his business.

And the way he did his son Ace by shipping him to work for the rest of his life like a slave.

"It doesn't matter!" Mason said, waving a hand dressed in a sparkling diamond watch.

"Yes it does! Once we get on those boats it will all be destroyed." He pointed at the burning land. Fire riding dry brush hopped one treetop to the next like squirrels. "Why do bad things keep happening to me? I really want to know."

It was clear that he wasn't leaving until he got his answer. So Mason did his best to give him a response. Hunching his shoulders he said, "I don't know. But you can build all this shit back."

"That's not enough!"

"Well it's going to have to be, nigga. Because I'm not going to lose you and our family worrying about a

287

property that you can rebuild. You've done it before, and you can do it again. Have you forgotten about Skull Island?"

He did.

Besides, in his mind it wasn't the same.

"I will never be able to rebuild this shit." Banks looked at him and Mason couldn't be sure because the heat was starting to consume him, but he swore he saw his eyes watering up. "Ever!"

Banks felt that deeply in all areas of his soul. For years he poured everything he had into the land. Making sure the blue crystal water was treasured by not allowing waste or any byproducts to be thrown in it.

By making sure the sand was cleaned and cared for four times a week by rakes.

By making sure the trees were watered and nurtured during the times the rain didn't come as planned.

And then there was his home.

He had a say so in every design element in his mansion. There wasn't a room, or a piece of furniture that didn't have his signature. Even his adult children's abodes were matters of the heart.

He adored that island and leaving it in the condition that it was now, in which fire consumed all, hurt like a mothafucka.

"Who did this shit?" Banks said through clenched teeth. "I don't get it."

"Except you do get it." Mason said, stepping a bit closer, his eyes penetrating his soul. "Don't you?"

Suddenly Spacey, Minnesota, Sugar, Blakeslee, Patrick, Bolt, and Riot walked up. All their gazes were in the same direction.

The blaze.

Minnesota and Spacey had gone into the house and gotten Riot and Sugar, who was safe in Blakeslee's arms.

Mason was relieved.

"What happened?" Blakeslee said doing too much. "Who could have done this shit? Why do they hate us?"

Spacey pinched her quiet.

"We all know who did this." Banks said in a low voice.

The five guilty ones looked at one another and back at him.

"Uh...who...who you think it is, pops?" Spacey asked.

"It was Ace. It's always Ace."

Of course it was him. Spacey thought. Why hadn't he thought of that before?

He was the perfect scapegoat.

Spacey looked at him and the other guilty ones and said, "I think you're right. That little nigga has always been known to start shit."

"Does this mean we aren't leaving anymore?" Patrick asked Mason.

"What?" Mason's gaze was still on the fire.

"You told us to pack. Are we not going to the States now?"

He focused on them. "No. We aren't going back."

Patrick and Bolt looked at each other. It appeared the Shaman's plan worked and so they smiled.

"We will be fine," Mason said. "Trust me. We will make it out of this shit."

"I hope so," Banks added.

Just at that moment Ace landed on a runway some miles away from the mansion in Belize.

Walid, upon seeing the fire down below, landed on a tiny runway south of Wales Island instead.

"Did you see that shit?" Walid whispered to himself mostly.

"Yes, sir," his copilot said. "Your island is on fire. I'm so sorry."

Four black Mercedes Sprinter vans rushed the Wales and Lou families to a luxury hotel in Belize. They had just gotten off four Go-Fast boats after leaving Wales Island.

Go-Fast boats were normally used to transport cocaine.

Today they were being used to transport billionaires.

Now in the vans, they were being covered in the first Sprinter by armed men and the last Sprinter by armed men.

Inside the second Sprinter to the front sat Banks, Mason, Faye, Minnesota, Sugar, Blakeslee, Spacey and Joey.

The third Sprinter, behind theirs, held the newly reunited Triad, Riot, Bolt and Patrick. Their handlers were also present to guard over the boys.

The silence was deafening.

When they left the island, flames had engulfed 30% of the land. If they were going to survive, they needed to leave expeditiously.

And that's what they did.

After instructing Faye to contact security to get them off Wales Island, and to set up their hotel, paid for in cryptocurrency, they grabbed only their most prized possessions and important documents.

When they rushed out of the mansion to connect to the boats, Banks played over and over in his mind one fact he thought he would never have to face.

And that was even though he was a billionaire, he still couldn't stop a forest fire from eating his shit.

In the back of the van Minnesota sat on one side of Blakeslee while Spacey sat on the other side of her. Staring at her intensely.

While they hated her ass, she was thinking of plans to make Mason Louisville fall hopelessly in love. Since she couldn't be a respected Wales, she would carry the Louisville name, she was certain.

"What's wrong with y'all?" Blakeslee whispered.

Minnesota looked up at Mason to be sure he wasn't looking and back at her before pinching her leg hard.

"Ouch, what did—."

Her words were stopped by Spacey's hand to her mouth.

Blakeslee looked at Minnesota and then Spacey.

Slowly he removed his hand and whispered in her ear. "I know you fucked Mason."

Her eyes widened and her gut churned.

Minnesota leaned over to her other ear. "And when we get settled, you will find a reason to leave this family."

Her eyes started to water. "But he's the older one," she whispered. "Why do I have to go?"

"Because they will never not be a thing." Minnesota schooled her. "And you will always start shit in this family." She looked down. "Just like me when I was your age." She took a deep breath. "Don't get me wrong, you can change. But you need hard lessons before you can even start."

Blakeslee took a deep breath and looked down. "They always blame the woman." At the same time, she had no intentions of going anywhere.

Suddenly Banks turned his head to focus on his children. "Y'all good back there."

"Yeah, pops." Spacey said, smooshing Blakeslee to threaten her to silence.

"You good too, Blakeslee?"

Her eyes widened. It was the first time he ever showed care for her. "Yes…I'm fine."

He turned back around.

Mason took a deep breath and focused on his friend. "Are you good?"

Banks nodded. "I left my fucking phone."

Mason shook his head. "Me too."

"This is the beginning of something else, Mason. What that new chapter is I don't know."

Sitting with baby Sugar in her lap, Faye looked over at the two friends and gazed downward.

"Whatever it is, we can handle it." Mason said.

Faye wanted to cry.

An hour later the family was settled into eight suites at the top of Ocean Lane Resorts. To ensure no more harm would come to his people, he made sure the top floor was only accessible to his family and employees.

The Triad shared a suite, Mason had one and Banks and his wife also had one. Minnesota had hers as well as Spacey, Joey and Blakeslee each having their own.

The eighth suite was for security who alternated duty.

At the moment, however, Faye was alone because Mason and Banks were going over plans for the future, in the event the mansion completely burned to the ground.

Which it looked like it would because the Belizean fire department had trouble beating the flames since Wales Island was isolated.

After tiring of being alone, and being ignored by Banks when she called, she left her room. But halfway down the hallway the door opened, and she was snatched inside by a strange man.

It was Paulo.

He along with the armed guards were there to fake protect Banks. Had Banks not been so taken aback by the fire, he would have noticed that the only man he actually knew was the driver in his Sprinter.

All the other men worked for Ace.

There was nothing like a fire to catch a man slipping.

Faye was about to scream until she saw Ace standing before her and Arbella sitting on the sofa.

At that moment Ace looked just like Banks. Starting with the blond streaks in his hair which he colored silver. And more than anything, Banks' gait which he studied incessantly.

Also in the room was Sharon who was holding Minnesota's dog whom Sharon was concerned would get burned alive had it stayed.

"Let her go, Paulo," Ace said.

He released Faye.

"What are you doing, Ace?" She trembled. "And why do you look like Banks?"

He looked back at Arbella and said, "Go in the room. I'll be there in a second."

She rolled her eyes and did as he demanded.

"So you were just going to ignore me forever?"

"Ace, I didn't know–."

"You didn't know you were going to marry my father? You didn't know that you would share his bed? Which part are you talking about?"

"You left me! And then he reached out to me to help with the app. For Kordell. One thing led to another and–."

"You fucked him! My ex-girlfriend fucked my father."

"Ace, that is not fair. It wasn't serious between us. You told me that repeatedly to my face."

He chuckled. "The crazy part is he called you and didn't even remember that I was the one who introduced you two. We used to spend hours going over capital ventures. Funding. And even apps. He wasn't too interested in apps at first until Kordell needed a hustle. And then who was the first person he reached out to? My bitch."

She started crying. "I thought he knew who I was too. But I think you fucked his head up so much that he didn't connect things. I even tried to ignore him when he first reached out about Kordell's app. But he–."

"Offered you more money."

She lowered her head. "Yes. Please don't–."

"Don't what? Tell him that you were the one who hacked into his banks for me before he took the money back? Or that you were the one who created spyware to siphon small amounts of his cash at a time? Or that before I met my girl, you were so into me that you used to sleep with my dick in your mouth?"

"I...I don't know what–."

"You foul. But you gonna make it up to me."

"How?"

He removed his shirt, and his body had every tattoo that Banks had on his skin. Despite being much younger, with pitch black shades and a rehearsed gait, he could definitely pass for him.

"I am going to take over his life."

"What...what are you talking about? It–."

"And you're going to help me."

"I already did what you wanted me to do today. I called you so you could send your men. I made the reservation for the hotel and gave you keys to their suites like you asked. What else do you fucking want from me?"

"You will transfer every dollar that my father has to another account."

"That...that will be impossible. It will cause all kinds of alerts to sound off."

"Then you better figure out a plan. Don't worry. I have full trust in you."

She swallowed the lump in her throat. "Then what will happen to me?"

"Well, Banks is married. So that means I'll need a wife."

She shook her head slowly. "So...so Arbella will assume my identity too?" She cried softly.

"You were the one who married him. Now you're mixed into the situation. There's no way out."

"Then what will happen next?"

"You change your identity. Remain in my employ. And I'll let you live. If you buck me though, you die tonight."

The floor to ceiling windows sparkled as Banks took in the beauty of Belize.

It wasn't Wales Island, but it would do.

The moon shone over the ocean causing it to glow in the distance. The dancing trees brought Banks a serenity that he didn't know he needed in that moment.

Turning around he looked at Mason, Spacey, Minnesota, and Joey. They were worried and waited for him to say something great.

After all, Banks always had an answer. Did he have one now?

"We are entering a new chapter. And we are going to have to work hard to keep each other strong."

"Agreed," Mason said firmly.

"But we can–."

Suddenly the door opened, and Ace entered with Arbella and six armed men. Their first order of duty was putting a bullet into Banks' most loyal guard.

Paulo fired right into his gut.

He dropped on the floor.

As they looked at his blood pour from his body Banks trembled with rage.

In fear Minnesota said, "He looks like pops. Moving like him too. What the fuck?"

"This nigga just won't die," Spacey said throwing his hands up.

"Hey, brother," Ace grinned.

"Fuck do you want with us now, nigga?" Spacey yelled. "Just leave us the fuck alone! Damn!"

Ace's men stepped in front of his family members, with weapons aimed in their direction. "You'll find out soon enough." He paused and nodded at his men who removed hoods from their pockets. "Everybody on the floor! Now!"

They obeyed, backs against the open window.

Banks said, "My men will come in this-."

"*My* men." Ace corrected. "The nigga we dropped was the only one who chose to stay loyal to you. Look at where that got him."

Banks was heated.

Mason had tried to warn him but he didn't listen.

"Don't do this, son," Mason begged. "There is still time to turn things around. Reconnect with family."

"But if you do this, whatever this is, it's done," Banks said. "And you will not win."

For a second Ace looked at his family sitting on the living room floor, mostly afraid for their lives. Something shifted in the pit of his stomach. Was this the right thing?

Because if he made a move, it would be like drawing a blood line in the sand.

"This nigga don't give a fuck about us," Spacey said, breaking his thought process. "He can suck my dick for all I care."

Mason, knowing Ace was possibly coming around in that moment, shook his head. "You should have stayed quiet, Spacey." He whispered.

Ace nodded to his men to move closer with the bags for their heads.

"So you're just gonna kidnap a whole billion-dollar family?" Banks asked.

"Kidnapping? You're adults. This a straight up snatching!"

Within seconds all of their heads were covered with satchels, snuffing out the moonlight.

Walid, Aliyah, and Baltimore were driving on the way to the hotel when he received a call from an unknown person with a quivering voice.

"Who is this?"

Aliyah looked on in fear, wondering the same.

"It's a friend of the family. I can't give you my name. I want you to know you do not want to come to the resort. Your family is being held hostage by Ace and his men. They need help. I'll reach back out when I can. Just know you have an ally."

When the call ended he took a deep breath.

"Who was that?" Aliyah asked.

"Ace...Ace has pops and father. He has all of them."

She covered her mouth. "Oh my God what are you going to do?"

"I knew this day would come." He said confidently. "So I already got a plan."

CARTEL PUBLICATIONS

PRESENTS

The Cartel Publications Order Form

www.thecartelpublications.com

Inmates **ONLY** receive novels for $12.00 per book **PLUS** shipping fee **PER BOOK.**

(Mail Order **MUST** come from inmate directly to receive discount)

Shyt List 1	_____	$15.00
Shyt List 2	_____	$15.00
Shyt List 3	_____	$15.00
Shyt List 4	_____	$15.00
Shyt List 5	_____	$15.00
Shyt List 6	_____	$15.00
Pitbulls In A Skirt	_____	$15.00
Pitbulls In A Skirt 2	_____	$15.00
Pitbulls In A Skirt 3	_____	$15.00
Pitbulls In A Skirt 4	_____	$15.00
Pitbulls In A Skirt 5	_____	$15.00
Victoria's Secret	_____	$15.00
Poison 1	_____	$15.00
Poison 2	_____	$15.00
Hell Razor Honeys	_____	$15.00
Hell Razor Honeys 2	_____	$15.00
A Hustler's Son	_____	$15.00
A Hustler's Son 2	_____	$15.00
Black and Ugly	_____	$15.00
Black and Ugly As Ever	_____	$15.00
Ms Wayne & The Queens of DC **(LGBTQ)**	_____	$15.00
Black And The Ugliest	_____	$15.00
Year Of The Crackmom	_____	$15.00
Deadheads	_____	$15.00
The Face That Launched A Thousand Bullets	_____	$15.00
The Unusual Suspects	_____	$15.00
Paid In Blood	_____	$15.00
Raunchy	_____	$15.00
Raunchy 2	_____	$15.00
Raunchy 3	_____	$15.00
Mad Maxxx (4ᵗʰ Book Raunchy Series)	_____	$15.00
Quita's Dayscare Center	_____	$15.00
Quita's Dayscare Center 2	_____	$15.00
Pretty Kings	_____	$15.00
Pretty Kings 2	_____	$15.00
Pretty Kings 3	_____	$15.00
Pretty Kings 4	_____	$15.00
Silence Of The Nine	_____	$15.00
Silence Of The Nine 2	_____	$15.00

Silence Of The Nine 3	_____	$15.00
Prison Throne	_____	$15.00
Drunk & Hot Girls	_____	$15.00
Hersband Material **(LGBTQ)** _ _____		$15.00
The End: How To Write A _____		$15.00
Bestselling Novel In 30 Days (Non-Fiction Guide)		
Upscale Kittens	_____	$15.00
Wake & Bake Boys	_____	$15.00
Young & Dumb	_____	$15.00
Young & Dumb 2: Vyce's Getback _____		$15.00
Tranny 911 **(LGBTQ)**	_____	$15.00
Tranny 911: Dixie's Rise **(LGBTQ)** _____		$15.00
First Comes Love, Then Comes Murder _____		$15.00
Luxury Tax	_____	$15.00
The Lying King	_____	$15.00
Crazy Kind Of Love	_____	$15.00
Goon	_____	$15.00
And They Call Me God	_____	$15.00
The Ungrateful Bastards	_____	$15.00
Lipstick Dom **(LGBTQ)**	_____	$15.00
A School of Dolls **(LGBTQ)**	_____	$15.00
Hoetic Justice	_____	$15.00
KALI: Raunchy Relived	_____	$15.00
(5th Book in Raunchy Series)		
Skeezers		$15.00
Skeezers 2	_____	$15.00
You Kissed Me, Now I Own You	_____	$15.00
Nefarious	_____	$15.00
Redbone 3: The Rise of The Fold	_____	$15.00
The Fold (4th Redbone Book) _____		$15.00
Clown Niggas	_____	$15.00
The One You Shouldn't Trust _____		$15.00
The WHORE The Wind		
Blew My Way	_____	$15.00
She Brings The Worst Kind	_____	$15.00
The House That Crack Built	_____	$15.00
The House That Crack Built 2 _____		15.00
The House That Crack Built 3 _____		$15.00
The House That Crack Built 4 _____		$15.00
Level Up **(LGBTQ)**	_____	$15.00
Villains: It's Savage Season	_____	$15.00
Gay For My Bae	_____	$15.00
War	_____	$15.00
War 2: All Hell Breaks Loose _____		$15.00
War 3: The Land Of The Lou's	_____	$15.00
War 4: Skull Island	_____	$15.00
War 5: Karma	_____	$15.00
War 6: Envy	_____	$15.00
War 7: Pink Cotton	_____	$15.00
Madjesty vs. Jayden (Novella) _____		$8.99
You Left Me No Choice	_____	$15.00
Truce – A War Saga (War 8)	_____	$15.00
Ask The Streets For Mercy	_____	$15.00
Truce 2 (War 9)	_____	$15.00
An Ace and Walid Very, Very Bad Christmas (War 10) ___		$15.00
Truce 3 – The Sins of The Fathers (War 11) _____		$15.00
Truce 4: The Finale (War 12) _____		$15.00
Treason	_____	$20.00
Treason 2	_____	$20.00
Hersband Material 2 **(LGBTQ)** _____		$15.00
The Gods Of Everything Else (War 13) _____		$15.00
The Gods Of Everything Else 2 (War 14) _____		$15.00

Treason 3	_____	$15.99
An Ugly Girl's Diary	_____	$15.99
The Gods Of Everything Else 3 (War 15)	_____	$15.99

(**Redbone 1 & 2** are **NOT** Cartel Publications novels and if <u>ordered</u> the cost is **FULL** price of $16.00 **each plus shipping. No Exceptions.**)

Please add **$7.00** for shipping and handling fees for up to **(2) BOOKS PER ORDER**. (INMATES INCLUDED) (See next page for details)

The Cartel Publications * P.O. BOX 486 OWINGS MILLS MD 21117

Name: _____

Address: _____

City/State: _____

Contact/Email: _____

Please allow 10-15 BUSINESS days Before shipping.

PLEASE NOTE DUE TO <u>COVID-19</u> SOME ORDERS MAY TAKE UP TO <u>3 WEEKS</u> OR LONGER BEFORE THEY SHIP

*The Cartel Publications is **NOT** responsible for <u>Prison Orders</u> rejected!*

NO RETURNS and NO REFUNDS
<u>NO PERSONAL CHECKS ACCEPTED</u>
STAMPS NO LONGER ACCEPTED